STARGÅTE
SG·1™

THE ILLUSTRATED COMPANION
SEASONS 1 AND 2

D1552700

STARGATE SG-1: THE ILLUSTRATED COMPANION
SEASONS 1 AND 2
1 84023 354 0

Published by
Titan Books
A division of
Titan Publishing Group Ltd
144 Southwark St
London
SE1 0UP

First edition August 2001
4 6 8 10 9 7 5

Stargate SG-1: The Illustrated Companion Seasons 1 and 2 © 2001 MGM Television Entertainment Inc. All rights reserved.
Stargate SG-1 ™ and © 2001 MGM Television Entertainment Inc. All rights reserved.

DEDICATION

This book is dedicated to Philip, Kerry and my very own SG one — Stuart.

ACKNOWLEDGEMENTS

Firstly, this book could never have been written without the generosity of spirit, time and talent donated by the amazing people involved in the production of *Stargate SG-1*. I offer each and every one my heartfelt thanks. Next, my gratitude goes to Adam Newell and Jo Boylett at Titan for displaying the patience of saints and to Richard Pasco, who not only kept me sane but jumped in to help write the synopses for season two's episode guides when there were no more hours left for me to use. A special hug goes to Katy Deery for her moral support and sense of humour, and to Richard Atkinson for his confidence in my abilities and for putting up with my whining. Most of all I'd like to thank Carol Marks George and Kim Cowan in Vancouver whose warmth, patience, professional assistance and enthusiasm has never wavered during the whole time I've been fortunate enough to be associated with this show. Some day all publicists will be like this.
—Thomasina Gibson

Titan Books would like to thank Charlie Clementson, Kobie Jackson and James Leland at MGM for their help with this project. Thanks also go to Richard Pasco for supplying the pictures from Gatecon 2000.

What did you think of this book? We love to hear from our readers. Please e-mail us at: readerfeedback@titanemail.com or write to Reader Feedback at the address above.

Titan Books are available from all good bookshops or direct from our mail order service. For a free catalogue or to order, phone 01858 433169 with your credit card details, e-mail asmltd@btinternet.com or write to Titan Books Mail Order, Bowden House, 36 Northampton Road, Market Harborough, Leics, LE16 9HE. Please quote reference SG/C1.

No part of this publication may be reproduced, stored in a retrieval system, or transmitted, in any form or by any means without the prior written permission of the publisher, nor be otherwise circulated in any form of binding or cover other than that in which it is published and without a similar condition being imposed on the subsequent purchaser.

A CIP catalogue record for this title is available from the British Library.

Printed and bound in Great Britain by MPG, Bodmin, Cornwall.

STARGATE
SG·1™

THE ILLUSTRATED COMPANION
SEASONS 1 AND 2

Thomasina Gibson

Stargate SG-1 developed for television by
Brad Wright & Jonathan Glassner

TITAN BOOKS

Contents

Foreword

When you're executive producer of a successful television show you've got a lot of people to thank. This is a collaborative medium; literally hundreds of people contribute to the success of *Stargate SG-1*. Since Thomasina has given me the opportunity, I thought I'd thank, in no particular order, a few of the people who make the show you like enough to buy this book.

James Tichenor, our visual effects producer. Every time you see a Goa'uld mothership, or exploding star, James and his team have spent hours upon hours working to make the effect as real and exciting as possible. I can't even count the many times he has worked through the night to perfect a shot.

Richard Hudolin is our production designer. My very first meeting every season is with Richard and his art director, Bridget McGuire, to help plan the upcoming stories. Never so often in my career have I walked onto sets that were more spectacular than I imagined when writing the story. Robert and Mark Davidson, our set decorators, work tirelessly to complete the picture, and Mark usually takes me for a few dollars every weekend on the golf course.

Christina McQuarrie designs our costumes. When I'm writing or re-writing a script I'll occasionally have to come in very early in the morning... I mean very early. Often the only other light on in the building is in Christina's office. She and her team absolutely astound me in their ability to create the wardrobe for entire alien civilisations. Peter Woeste and Jim Menard alternate as our directors of photography. Their work is a huge part of why our show looks so good, especially with the addition of Will Waring as camera operator.

Peter DeLuise does everything from directing, to writing, to playing more cameo roles than anyone. I've often joked that I made Peter a creative consultant just to get him out of my office and into his own. He contributes so much, with so much humour, that he is a joy to work with. Martin Wood has directed some of our best episodes, and is an integral part of our creative team. More important than that, we flew T-38s together in Texas last summer.

Since their arrival in season four, writers Paul Mullie and Joseph Mallozzi have breathed new life into *Stargate SG-1*, and in so doing, saved mine. They're talented, fast, and they're very funny. Humour is everything when you work together for twelve hours a day. (Or in Joe's case, several hours a day.) Please, nobody tell them just how good they really are until I've retired.

Michael Greenburg is even funnier. Just wait until you read the

Foreword he's written for the second volume of *Stargate SG-1: The Illustrated Companion*. Now that's funny. Michael and I have been partners from the beginning, and I would love to say how much I've enjoyed working with him, and learned from him, but I know he'd much rather I mention he's really funny.

Richard Dean Anderson is not just the name above the title; he's one of our executive producers. I will forever be grateful to him for not being a three hundred-pound gorilla. John Smith defines the word 'producer' by doing nothing less than make this show happen. Along with Andy Mikita and John Lenic, he manages to put more on the screen for the money than any other show I've been a part of. Jonathan Glassner and I created this show together. I learned a lot of what I know about how to make a television show from Jon.

Cath-Anne Ambrose is the story department assistant or, as she likes to call herself, 'Script Diva'. Robert Cooper is in many ways the heart and soul of *Stargate*. He's written the most episodes, come up with the most ideas, and grown to fill Jonathan's shoes as executive producer. The phrase 'I could never have done this without him' is an understatement. He is also very funny.

Above: Brad Wright.

There are many more people who deserve thanks, especially our fabulous cast, but for once, I wanted to mention those behind the scenes who make this show work. So for myself, I have to include my wife Deb, and my daughters Tessa and Kayla. I couldn't go to work with a smile on my face if I didn't have them to come home to.

Finally, I'd like to thank Thomasina Gibson for this book. She once told me, years ago when we were just starting out, that she knew *Stargate* would be a success. I'm glad she was right.

Brad Wright
Executive Producer/Co-creator *Stargate SG-1*
May 2001

Initiating the Cycle

MGM statement, 1997

"A gateway to the imagination has been opened and a new universe of action and adventure has been unleashed."

When *Stargate* the motion picture set the big screen alight in 1994, it also fired the imaginations of Jonathan Glassner and Brad Wright, who thought the idea of using an ancient portal to travel to a world far beyond our own intriguing to say the least. "I liked the original movie," admits Wright. "But I felt there was so much more to explore in terms of storytelling. For instance, what if the Stargate could be used to travel to many other places? What if we found the means to choose those destinations? What if we encountered other races and what might we learn from them?"

Jonathan Glassner takes up the story. "On a rainy Vancouver day in winter 1996, John Symes, the then president of MGM Worldwide Television, flew to the set of *The Outer Limits*, which I was executive producing at the time. He came to convince me to stay on the show for another season. I had been away from California for three years and wanted to go home. He asked me if there was anything else I wanted to do that would keep me up there. I told him that MGM had a movie in their library called *Stargate*, which I thought would make a great TV series. I said I would consider staying if I could create that show for television and produce it. His response was vague (for various legal, financial and political reasons, he wasn't sure he could do it). He went back to Los Angeles and I figured that was the end of that.

"Little did I know that John had posed the same question to Brad Wright (who was also working on *The Outer Limits*). And, independently of me, Brad had made the same request — he wanted to do *Stargate* for television.

"Cut to a month later. John Symes returns to Vancouver to meet with Brad and me. He called us into an office, closed the door, and said simply, 'How would you two feel about doing a *Stargate* series together?' Brad and I were thrilled by the idea. We enjoyed working together on *The Outer Limits* and loved the idea of doing *Stargate* together. We both knew that it was going to be a huge undertaking and the thought of sharing the burden was appealing. Only one more issue remained — I told John that it must be understood up front that the show was going to be very expensive to produce. 'Not a problem, within reason,' he said. That's what John had been doing the past month — putting together a brilliant business plan involv-

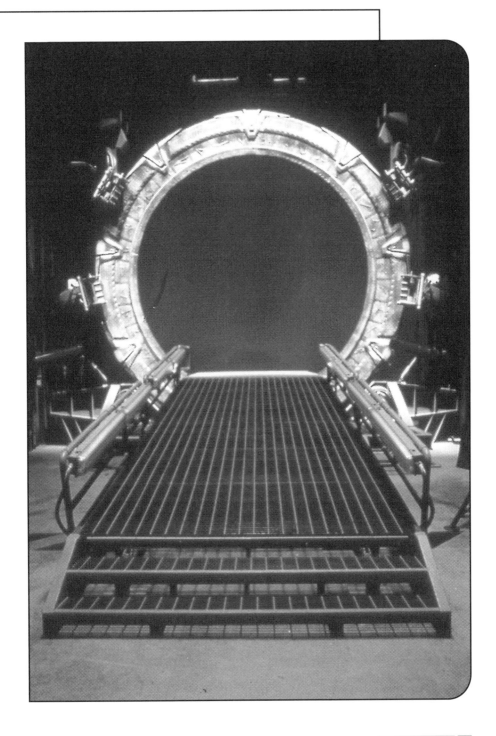

ing two US networks, a large US station group, and huge international sales to pay for the show. He had already made it possible. Now all we had to do was make it a reality."

Having initiated the cycle, Symes set about persuading Richard Dean Anderson, a friend and colleague from their days working together on *MacGyver*, to come on board. "John called me and said, 'I really want you to do this,'" recalls Anderson. "He sent me the tape so I watched the movie a few times, did my research and saw the potential of the movie as a great starting block for the series." The Jack O'Neill character also intrigued the actor: "He's a man trained to obey orders, but with the need to follow his own moral compass. I thought it would be interesting to draw out his humanity and sense of humour in situations where he's under pressure." Before embarking on his journey through the Stargate, Anderson made sure that everyone understood he would portray Colonel O'Neill his way, and inject the character with many of his own little foibles: "I have a very irreverent sense of humour. It's very dry, sarcastic, naughty, and I wanted to give O'Neill that kind of levity. Fortunately, they went along with me." *Stargate SG-1* afforded Anderson the chance to work with long-time business partner Michael Greenburg. "It had been some time since we'd worked on a television series together," Anderson remembers, "and we really wanted to do that. Thankfully, *Stargate* provided the perfect opportunity."

"What I liked about the idea, apart from working with Rick," agrees Greenburg, "was that here we had a science fiction premise that also had some basis in reality. Our Stargate Command, the SGC, is part of Space Command, which is an actual division of the United States Air Force. Our stories, in keeping with the mythology established in the movie, involve humans who were taken by alien invaders thousands of years ago and forced to act as slaves for, or 'hosts' to the Goa'uld." Greenburg feels much of *Stargate SG-1*'s huge success is down to the writers, who have managed to incorporate these factual, human and science fiction elements into a show in which "our universe is restricted only by the limit of our imaginations."

The job of creating this fertile universe in a practical sense fell to production designer Richard Hudolin, who felt a bond with Glassner and Wright from the very start. Describing his first meeting with them, Hudolin recalls, "We got along very well personally and professionally we just 'clicked'. We each knew exactly what the others were thinking. There was no confusion as to where we were going. When you have designers and writers working together like that, everything is going to happen as it

should. We knew straight off that I could handle something the size and scope of the *Stargate SG-1* project. I started on my own almost straight away and worked for a couple of weeks to get the designs together for the pilot episode, during which time the other producers were coming on board and wrapping up the other side of the production process. I remember doing a presentation to a whole trailer-full of people, and they really bought into my designs for the Stargate Command sets."

Above: *An early publicity shot of the SG-1 team.*

At this point, Hudolin called in Thom Wells as construction co-ordinator and immediately hired an art department: "Basically a skeletal construction crew worked together with art director Bridget McGuire's 'magnificent seven' in the art department for around three weeks. We managed the shortest of breaks for Christmas 1996 before hiring 150 carpenters to just blast away at it to get the job done. It was an incredible push. A 'minor' consideration was that whatever sets we constructed had to be collapsible, because the permanent sound stages hadn't been built yet! We had to be able to move everything from the huge visual effects stage, which was over thirty-six feet high, across the lot and re-assemble it on the permanent soundstage, once it was ready." Hudolin recalls, "I had the builders from MGM asking, 'How big does this need to be?' and, 'What size do

Above: On location for 'Children of the Gods'.

you want this?' as the buildings were being erected. It was like getting in an aeroplane and taking off, knowing that as you're flying they are still building the landing strip!"

While this frenetic activity continued on set, a very long and laborious casting process was underway to find the other members of Jack O'Neill's team. Although he was clearly perfect for the part, the decision to cast Michael Shanks as Dr Daniel Jackson was far from easy. "We looked at around 500 men and finally narrowed it down to three that we thought were all very strong choices," Jonathan Glassner remembers. "We were torn, because all three actors had great strengths and they were all very different, but we just had a feeling, though we didn't even really see it in the audition, that Michael could do comedy. I think he was a little nervous at the audition, but we kept thinking, 'There's something about this guy. He's got a wit about him.' Then when shooting began, and the 'dailies' started coming in, we all went 'Thank God!'"

Shanks recalls that, even though none of them knew they would be offered parts at the time, there was an immediate bond between the actors who would become the SG-1 team: 'We were sitting there at the audition,

Above: Apophis's Serpent Guard, as seen in 'Children of the Gods'.

just talking away and going through the process, but there was something special between us. It was kind of funny, but great, walking on set the first day and seeing the same faces. It just felt right."

Brad Wright maintains he and Glassner were insistent from the start that Amanda Tapping was the woman for the job of breathing life into Samantha Carter: "We had a massive hunt for this cast but really, really wanted Amanda for the role." Their enthusiasm was not met with unanimous approval at first, but within five episodes, Tapping's determined portrayal of, as she puts it, "a scientist smack in the middle of an adventurous boys' club" received an overwhelming vote of confidence from all concerned. Glassner smiles, "We got a call saying, 'OK, guys, you were right. We would have been in trouble if we had cast anyone else in that part.'"

"Sam can hang with the men and do anything that's asked of her," Tapping says. "She's smart, determined, adventurous and definitely not afraid of a little excitement. I'm very similar to her in that way."

"When Christopher Judge walked in the room, before he said a word we went 'OK — that's him!'" laughs Wright. His co-executive producer adds, "When Chris walked in I leaned over to Brad and whispered,

'Please, God, let him be able to act!' Then he read the part, did a great job and made Teal'c his own. We really lucked out with our cast."

In addition to their quality cast, the executive producers felt blessed to have the skills of producer John Smith to help deliver a high quality of production, whilst keeping an eye on the budget. The man himself modestly proclaims that he's only as good as the people around him. "If you surround yourself with great people they'll make you look good! I wander around looking like I know what the hell I'm doing, but it's really down to the team effort everyone else puts in," Smith insists. "My job is to get the episode shot. When I first get a script I think, 'Ohmigod! How am I going to pull this off?' But then you get talking to, and working with, the other people and by the time we come to shoot, most of the difficulties have already been worked out. The name of the game for us is to get as much money as possible in *front* of the camera, and that takes a lot of planning on everyone's part. You know that if you lose even a day's shooting it's 75,000 US dollars out the door just in crew labour alone, and that money doesn't get in front of the camera." Looking back, Smith admits, "At the start of the first year we were scrambling around because we were pretty much up to the limit of the budget, but by the beginning of season two we were in pretty good shape. We figured out better and quicker ways to do things, and managed to refine the process in terms of where we go with ideas, the sets we build, the locations we choose. A lot of people put in a tremendous amount of effort to make sure *Stargate SG-1* became a really smooth-running operation. I'm really proud that we've managed to deliver the show eleven days ahead of schedule for the past three years.

"In fact," grins Smith, "you can almost set your clock by us. On normal days we come in at 7am and go home at 7pm. It's kind of a joke on set that with *Stargate* three things in life are guaranteed: you're going to start at 7am, your pay cheque won't bounce and, when you've lived to a ripe old age, you're going to die."

Whilst the production of *Stargate SG-1* usually runs smoothly, John Smith remembers a particular time during the second year when it was quite a different story. "Richard Dean Anderson's daughter was due, but none of us had any idea when she would make her first appearance. So I'm chewing my nails because we were going to give Rick the time off at a moment's notice, whenever he needed to go to the hospital. Wylie is the most important thing that has ever happened in his life, which is how it should be, and we all supported that. But it was a major scheduling problem, because babies arrive when they are ready, and we actually had to rewrite four different episodes to accommodate this, as we kept expecting

Rick to be gone. The due date was in July, and we had an episode to finish two days later so we thought, 'OK, we'll write him out of that.' But the baby didn't appear, so we wrote him out of the next episode, but she still didn't arrive. We then had a hiatus for two weeks, and breathed huge sighs of relief because we thought she'd be born during the holiday for sure. She wasn't, and everyone was getting pretty jumpy. It was getting so we didn't dare risk putting Rick in major scenes, but miraculously Wylie had the grace to be born on the weekend before the next episode, so Rick never actually conceded a day's shooting."

Co-executive producer and writer Robert C. Cooper fondly remembers the first two seasons of the show as the time when quite a few risks were being taken: "We were finding our feet and exploring new avenues, and I'd say we got it right about fifty per cent of the time. We produced some of our best ever episodes during those seasons, but even our less than spectacular efforts provided valuable lessons for us to work on. It was an interesting rollercoaster of a ride for us, but by season three I feel we were almost there in terms of what would work best for the show." ⋏

Above: A concept drawing for the early first season episode 'The Broca Divide'.

Children of the Gods

Regular cast: Richard Dean Anderson (Colonel Jack O'Neill), Michael Shanks (Dr Daniel Jackson), Amanda Tapping (Captain Samantha Carter), Christopher Judge (Teal'c), Don S. Davis (General Hammond)

Written by: Jonathan Glassner and Brad Wright
Directed by: Mario Azzopardi

Guest cast: Jay Acovone (Major Charles Kawalsky), Vaitiare Bandera (Sha're), Robert Wisden (Major Samuels), Peter Williams (Apophis), Brent Stait (Major Ferretti), Gary Jones (Technician), Alex Cruz (Skaara)

Forced to reveal he denied an order to destroy Abydos, a planet he'd visited more than a year earlier via the Stargate, Colonel Jack O'Neill is recalled from retirement when a group of hostile aliens emerge through the ancient transportation portal now housed in an underground military facility on Earth. Infuriated that the aliens would dare to bring conflict to their doorstep, Stargate Command sends O'Neill, two former colleagues and a new team member, astrophysicist Captain Samantha Carter, to Abydos to discover the reason behind the attack. Reunited with Dr Daniel Jackson, now married to local girl Sha're, and O'Neill's adopted son Skaara, the team are awed by Jackson's latest discovery: a giant cartouche, a wealth of hieroglyphic-covered information, which appears to be a map of the Stargate system throughout the galaxy. But, before the team can celebrate the archaeologist's success, Apophis, the evil System Lord, kidnaps Skaara and Sha're. Battling to avoid being killed by the Goa'uld or being taken as hosts for the hideous snake creatures, SG-1 must save themselves and the Abydans before General Hammond sends a nuclear weapon to destroy the planet.

Hammond to O'Neill

"Have you thought about writing a book?"

"I've thought about it, but I'd have to shoot anybody that read it."

One outstanding memory lingers in the minds of everyone involved in the filming of Stargate SG-1's première episode, and that's "Rain!" "The first day of filming we had rain on a scale that was practically a national disaster," executive producer Brad Wright recalls, "talk about the wrath of the gods!"

"We had fifty extra cast members all in intricate costumes," says

make-up supervisor Jan Newman. "And we had prisoners all covered with dirt but, of course, it was meant to be dry dirt from a desert planet, not mud from a sodden British Columbia. Added to that, we had Apophis and Teal'c covered in gold dust, which meant they had to be kept completely dry and away from any surface which might mar the sheen on their skin." Given the ebullient nature of the two actors playing those characters, who, by all accounts, can't sit still for a minute, Newman grins, "It was a nightmare."

Above: Apophis enslaves an Air Force soldier.

Peter Williams says that wearing Apophis's armour "wasn't so much flying by the seat of your pants as flying by the tip of your nose. I had two different versions of the head-dress: one made of rubber which weighed around sixty pounds, and one where the visor moved up and down which weighed much more. The pneumatic one was doubly uncomfortable because it was operated by a man standing off-camera, and the whole thing came and went within a centimetre of the tip of my nose. My frame of reference was the back of the helmet. If my head touched it, I'd be ok. If not — it was 'look out' time!" ʌ

The Enemy Within

Written by: Brad Wright Directed by: Dennis Berry	Guest cast: Jay Acovone (Major Charles Kawalsky), Kevin McNulty (Dr Warner), Gary Jones (Technician), Alan Rachins (Colonel Kennedy), Warren Takeuchi (Young Doctor)

O'Neill needs to employ diplomatic as well as military skills in order to persuade the United States forces to accept Teal'c, an alien who risked his life to save the Colonel and his team, into their ranks. Understandably wary at first, General Hammond refuses to approve the appointment until military intelligence has had the opportunity to "debrief" the Jaffa. Whilst the suicidal forces of the Goa'uld continue to bombard the titanium alloy iris protecting the Stargate on Earth, O'Neill's problems increase with the news that the headaches plaguing his right-hand man, Kawalsky, are caused by an unfriendly larva that has attached itself to his brain. Teal'c proves his loyalty by assisting the doctors who have to try to remove the larva, and by preventing the emerging Goa'uld from escaping through the Stargate.

> **O'Neill to Kawalsky**
>
> "If you don't make it — can I have your stereo?"

Jay Acovone was thrilled but surprised when the call came to say he'd been offered the role of Kawalsky. "The casting director, Mary Jo Slater, called my agent and I went to the audition in the MGM building in Santa Monica," the actor remembers. "I did what I thought was a reasonably good job and went home. I figured that they'd be making a decision real soon, so when I didn't hear for a couple of weeks, I was disappointed, but put it down to experience and forgot about it. Then three

The Goa'uld

A parasitic race of worm-like creatures that burrow into and inhabit other life forms. Able to infest many kinds of beings, they have nevertheless found humans amongst the most plentiful and suitable races for their nefarious purposes. Starting off as an infant larva, the Goa'uld continues to grow inside the 'host' until maturity, when it is removed and introduced into a new recipient. The previous body is left to deteriorate and die, as the Goa'uld see these individuals simply as slaves or vessels.

weeks after I'd gone in, they called and said, 'We want you to play Kawalsky.' It was meant to be just one show — but I just keep popping up there." Asked if he had any thoughts on why his character got bumped off so early, the irrepressible Mr Acovone replies, "I was told that they wanted the guy who played him in the movie, but apparently he didn't want to do a series. They then said to him, 'How about if we kill Kawalsky off in the first show?' When I came on board, I told them I wanted to do a series very much, but the producers didn't have approval to do anything else, so I got killed off. That's my story and I'm sticking to it!"

Above: An infected Kawalsky makes for the Gate.

Despite his demise, Kawalsky comes back to haunt his old friend O'Neill in 'The Gamekeeper' and in season three's 'Point of View'. Having "had a blast" in the episodes he's done so far, all the effervescent Mr Acovone really wants to ask the writers is, "When am I coming back again?" Executive producer Robert Cooper reassuringly replies, "No one ever dies in science fiction." ᚥ

Emancipation

Written by: Katharyn Powers
Directed by: Jeff Woolnough

Guest cast: Cary-Hiroyuki Tagawa (Turghan), Jorge Vargas (Abu), Soon-Tek Oh (Moughal), Crystal Lo (Nya)

SG-1 travel to the planet Simarka and meet the Shavadai, a race of people who bear a remarkable resemblance to the ancient Mongols. Encouraged by Daniel to adopt a "when in Rome" policy, Sam Carter finds herself relegated to the role of second class citizen in a community where it is death for a woman to even speak without permission from a man. Uncomfortable intellectually and physically — she's forced to wear the ceremonial robes of the local women — Sam is further humiliated when the son of one chieftain tries to swap her for Nya, the daughter of an enemy. When the exchange is unsuccessful, Carter tries to aid the course of true love and female emancipation by arranging Nya's escape, only to face the girl's father in battle when the plans go awry.

Sam to Daniel

"Find me an anthropologist who dresses like this and I will eat this head-dress."

"I just remember that dress," shudders Amanda Tapping. Referring to the diaphanous blue affair which showed more than a suggestion of cleavage, she grins, "When the SG-1 guys and the crew first saw it they all went 'Woohoo!' I just looked at them and said, 'You know guys, smoke and mirrors, smoke and mirrors. There's a lot of push me-pull you working here.' That's all it ever was and is all it's ever going to be!"

According to executive producer Jonathan Glassner, 'Emancipation' was one of the episodes shot "whilst we were still finding our feet" and which showed the way *not* to go as far as the *Stargate SG-1* universe was concerned: "It was too preachy, and we quickly realised we shouldn't be that preachy. Science fiction is a very good medium for having little moral tales and subtle messages built into the stories, and that's what we were trying to do. We just went way too far with that one; so we pulled back afterwards." Amanda Tapping concurs: "Because none of us really liked the episode, I was feeling a little off base with it. Although I did enjoy doing the fight sequence, especially working with the stunt co-ordinator for three days to get it right." Tapping laughs that the sequence was actually payback time for a certain member of the cast: "The Mongol warrior who ends up buying my character was very tough. He had my throat in a really tight grip and grabbed my hair right back, but

Above: Carter defies convention.

then we had the fight sequence so I got my revenge."

Tapping says another source of amusement was actually caught on film: "There's a moment when we're running across a field because we hear screams, and if you watch, you can see us laughing. That field was full of potholes and we'd run over it so many times in rehearsal that we were absolutely knackered. Then, for no real reason, it just cracked us up that we were supposed to be this 'top flight commando unit' romping about in this field, and as we started running we forgot the cameras were rolling, and were still laughing. People have written to me about it. We got totally caught!" ⋏

The Broca Divide

Written by: Jonathan Glassner	**Guest cast:** Teryl Rothery (Dr Janet Fraiser), Gary
Directed by: William Gereghty	Jones (Technician), Gerard Plunkett (Councillor Tuplo),
	Danny Wattley (Johnson), Roxana Phillip (Melosha)

Arriving on a planet known simply as P3X797, the SG-1 team discover a world populated by some Bronze Age inhabitants (known as the Untouched) on the light side of the globe, whilst on the dark side they find a bunch of Neanderthals with limited skills and even baser instincts. Returning through the Stargate, the team, with the exception of Teal'c and Daniel, begin to display their baser instincts and start to develop the heavy brows of the Touched. And to make things worse, others at Stargate Command, including General Hammond, begin to display the same symptoms. Daniel and Teal'c are forced to reurn to P3X797, and discover that the reason for the changes is a mysterious virus which causes the host to regress to a Neanderthal-like state. It is left to the Jaffa, Dr Jackson and newcomer Dr Janet Fraiser to find an antidote to the horrifying disease before everyone on Cheyenne Mountain succumbs and the Stargate project is closed down.

SG-3 Marines to Daniel

"We'll watch your back side."

"It's my front side I'm worried about."

"When we first started on the series and were really just feeling it out, we were having a hard time trying to figure out what the tone of the show was, and which way we wanted to go with regard to certain elements. 'The Broca Divide' was one of our test shows," comments executive producer Jonathan Glassner. "The show was an attempt to have fun, and it's probably the closest to where we continued to go," he admits, also recalling that the episode was one of the first chances to properly sound out the actors' strengths. "What was really great was how thrilled we were with Richard Dean Anderson," he enthuses. "I had no idea what he was capable of, apart from the straight man stuff he does so well, but here he had to basically play a caveman. Richard did such a fantastic job, it made us start writing more things for him to do that were fun, and stretched him beyond what he's known for. I haven't asked him about it, but I think he appreciated that."

The episode also saw Teryl Rothery join the show. "Teryl played

a big part in 'The Broca Divide'," says Glassner, "and, though Brad and I had worked with her many times before, that was the first time we saw the chemistry between her and the others — especially between her and Rick. That was the episode that made us decide to make her a little more of a regular."

The relationship between Dr Fraiser and O'Neill is what makes 'The Broca Divide' one of Teryl Rothery's favourite episodes. "There were so many great moments for Janet where she got to show her strength of character, the depth of her compassion for her patients and her dedication to the SG teams," the actress recalls. "But my favourite scenes have to be the ones with Richard Dean Anderson, especially the one where he asks Janet to experiment on him."

Rothery is also delighted that a one-episode guest star spot turned into a regular occurrence: "My agent called and said I'd been offered a part in *Stargate SG-1*, though then very cautiously added, 'The character *may recur*.'" λ

Above: Carter and O'Neill, happy to be home.

The First Commandment

Written by: Robert C. Cooper
Directed by: Dennis Berry

Guest cast: William Russ (Captain Jonas Hansen), Roger R. Cross (Lieutenant Connor), Zahf Hajee (Jamala), Adrian Hughes (Lieutenant Baker), D. Neil Mark (Frakes)

Overtaken by delusions of grandeur, the commanding officer of SG-9 is terrorising the people of a distant planet into believing he is a god. Ruling the inhabitants without mercy, Captain Jonas Hanson demands the primitive cave dwellers rebuild the giant Goa'uld temples in his honour. Captain Carter, once romantically involved with the despot, thinks she can stop him. O'Neill reckons the best way is to storm his compound, but Daniel Jackson and Teal'c set out to convince the people of the planet that Hanson's power is man-made rather than divine, and that they can build their own future, physically and metaphorically, without the need for false gods.

Daniel to Sam

"This tastes like chicken."

"What's wrong with that?"

"It's macaroni cheese."

"Martin Wood made his début as first assistant director on this episode," states Brad Wright. "He did such a lot of great work that we began to trust Martin's instincts from the get-go." However, even Wood's talent couldn't lift the episode as high as the creative team would have liked. Wright goes on, "'The First Commandment' was a story that is not much of a fan favourite. I think it was a great idea, but not for one of the first six *Stargates*. In retrospect, it didn't make any sense that a guy could have a 'God' complex so early in the programme and, worse than that, would they have picked a candidate so poorly as to allow him to be that way? It's one of those episodes where we have to admit we'd bitten off more than we could chew. It was very expensive to produce, but doesn't really look like it. On the other hand, it was a major learning experience for us, and made us capable of making *Stargate SG-1* much better."

Robert C. Cooper confesses that 'The First Commandment' is his least favourite episode in season one: "Even though the story idea got me the job on *Stargate* in the first place, I feel there were better choices that could have been made." On reflection, Cooper thinks the idea of a past romance having a bearing on how Samantha Carter

would conduct herself in the field wasn't quite right for the character at that time. "I got a lot of feedback about that one," he smiles.

Above: O'Neill goes undercover.

"It was the first cheery moment that I got to play," says Amanda Tapping. "I remember doing this punch when I hit the guy and say, 'Well, that was refreshing.' Though when I did it, because of the way I had my gun slung at the time, it swung round and whacked me on the hip and I'm like, 'Wow! That hurts.' So it was kind of like karma. I hit someone, so I got hit back."

"That episode was another example where we were still trying to figure out what the hell sort of show *Stargate SG-1* was!" Jonathan Glassner suggests. ⋏

Cold Lazarus

Written by: Jeffery F. King Directed by: Kenneth J. Girotti	Guest cast: Teryl Rothery (Dr Fraiser), Harley Jane Kozak (Sara O'Neill), Gary Jones (Technician), Wally Dalton (Sara's Father), Kyle Graham (Charlie O'Neill)

There's double trouble when a being from P3X562 duplicates O'Neill and returns through the Stargate in his stead. Determined to find the Colonel's son Charlie, tragically killed some time before, the *doppelgänger* seeks out O'Neill's estranged wife, Sara, in an effort to find the boy, and help ease the pain he senses in the real O'Neill. Meanwhile, Sam and Daniel realise that the crystals they discovered on P3X562 are in fact 'bodies', housing the essence of a highly intelligent race almost obliterated by the Goa'uld. The beings explain that they cannot survive in the Earth's intense electromagnetic field, and that with continued exposure, the O'Neill double will become highly unstable and could self-destruct, putting Sara and others in great danger. When SG-1 finally catch up with him, the alien apologises for the distress he's caused and, in a touching gesture, assumes Charlie's form, allowing the boy's parents the chance to say goodbye.

Teal'c to Daniel

"Your world is strange."

"So's yours."

Although it may have looked as though the startlingly bright alien landscape of P3X562 was the result of some super visual effects, executive producer Michael Greenburg reveals that 'Cold Lazarus' was actually filmed in a sulphur pit. "We supplemented the colour with some matte painting," he explains, "but we did shoot on location and it really was very yellow. It was also very hard working in that pit, because the chemical just permeated the air." Laughing about the fact that sulphur can have a particularly noxious odour, Greenburg insists, "It didn't smell *that* bad when we were there. It's just that it was a very hot day, as I remember, and the combination of the terrain, the heat and the substance itself made life a bit of a challenge."

Greenburg recalls that there were challenges of another sort to overcome in the studio: "We did a lot of complex motion control camera work on that show, particularly with the shots of O'Neill's son, but we're really proud of the way it turned out."

Greenburg also remembers the episode as being one of the most emotional of the early seasons: "Rick was really into it, because it

went back into O'Neill's relationship with his son, and anytime you do something like that it's going to be emotional and very dramatic. Fortunately, it's a pretty light-hearted set and the director was a jokester, so he kept us going."

Above: Close encounters with a crystal on P3X562.

"There have been many wonderful episodes of *Stargate SG-1*," says Hank Cohen, the current president of MGM Television, "but 'Cold Lazarus' is the one that sticks in my memory. I remember when we took it to MIPCOM [an annual event to showcase new productions and concepts in television and film]. We were in one of the little sales offices showing it to buyers from the United Kingdom and Germany. I stepped out of the room for a moment — I'd already seen it eight million times — and when I came back five people in the room were in tears. I knew then that not only did we have a show that would appeal to 'slaves' to the sci-fi genre, but the humanity of our stories would appeal to anyone." ⅄

The Nox

Written by: Hart Hanson Directed by: Charles Correll	Guest cast: Peter Williams (Apophis), Armin Shimerman (Anteaus), Ray Xifo (Ohper), Gary Jones (Technician), Frida Betrani (Lya), Terry David Mulligan (Secretary of Defense David Swift), Addison Ridge (Nafrayu), Michasa Armstrong (Shak'l)

Whilst on a trip to seek out some creatures known as Fenri, which Teal'c remembers as having the power of invisibility, the SG-1 team get into a skirmish with a Goa'uld hunting party and are killed. Fortunately, a mystical group of fairy-like beings are on hand to weave their magic and revive the group. Amazed by their healing powers but concerned that their peaceful demeanour will attract more unwelcome attention from the Goa'uld, SG-1 offer US military might to defend the apparently defenceless little beings. The Nox once more surprise the team by revealing that they have their own solution to any attack, giving new credence to the proverb, 'The Meek shall inherit the Earth.'

O'Neill

"The very young do not always do as they are told."

Christopher Judge considers the place where the Nox dwell as one of his favourite planets. "If I had a choice in the matter I would definitely visit the place where the Nox live," he says. "They are special. In their gentle, positive way they taught us to ask 'who are we, in our egocentric

The Nox

A race of diminutive gentlefolk, the Nox are more akin to mystical forest creatures than human beings. Resembling Victorian faeries in appearance, they seem to inhabit a forest world, their attire and skin blending with the colours and textures that surround them. Although placid and docile most of the time, they have enormous strength of will, and can display great determination and resourcefulness when their peaceful philosophies are challenged. Possessing powers far greater than our own (at this stage in our development), they can appear and disappear at will, can provide a cloak of invisibility to whomsoever they choose and can re-introduce the life force into another being by pooling their chi with other members of the Nox community. Along with the Asgard, the Furling and the Tollan, they are the guardians of all that is good and productive in the universe.

Above: The Nox offer some gentle guidance.

way, to say how someone else should live or conduct their lives?' I thought that without beating everyone over the head with it, it was a great learning episode."

Colleague Michael Shanks feels there was another aspect to their learning experience: "Armin Shimerman was very much the mentor in more ways than one. Having been part of a long-running science fiction franchise [as Quark in *Star Trek: Deep Space Nine*], he had more experience than any of us in working through the various practical challenges this medium throws at you. He understood what we were trying to do in terms of building the mythology and quietly shared that experience with us. It was wonderful working with him."

It wasn't just sweetness and light on set that week. "I remember this episode significantly for one particular line," jokes Apophis's *alter ego*, the very benign Peter Williams. "It's directed towards Jack O'Neill and I yell, 'Fool! I will kill you!' Kind of ironic considering what happens a little later on in the series, but I particularly enjoyed delivering that line." ⋏

Brief Candle

Story by: Steven Barnes	Guest cast: Teryl Rothery (Dr Fraiser), Bobbie Phillips
Teleplay by: Katharyn Powers	(Kynthia), Harrison Coe (Alekos), Gabrielle Miller
Directed by: Mario Azzopardi	(Thetys), Gary Jones (Technician)

Although a doctor of archaeology rather than medicine, Daniel Jackson undertakes the role of midwife with considerable aplomb moments after SG-1 set foot on the planet Argos. Invited to attend the festivities to celebrate the resulting baby's birth, the team encounters a joyful community of beautiful people who hold hands a lot and party during the day, but collapse in a heap as soon as the sun goes down. Drugged and seduced by the stunning Kynthia, O'Neill wakes to find that not only is he suffering from a hangover and a serious case of 'the morning after the night before blues', but he is showing signs of rapid ageing. The SG-1 team learn that the Argosians themselves live very brief lives — their lifespan is only one hundred days.

O'Neill

"I was kinda looking forward to a little shuffle-board with the fellas."

Though O'Neill has been infected with the same thing which causes this accelerated life-cycle, it seems to be having a more exaggerated effect on him. Once they establish that the cause of the ageing is nanocytes — microscopic robots — in the Argosians' blood, part of a now-defunct Goa'uld experiment, the rest of the team must find a cure, or a way to turn the nanocytes off before O'Neill's time runs out. Meanwhile, they can only watch as he achieves octogenarian status before their very eyes.

Make-up supervisor Jan Newman declares 'Brief Candle' one of her most satisfying projects. "The characters were aged from forty-five to one hundred years old in seven stages," she explains. "The first three stages (fifty, fifty-five and sixty-five) were achieved without prosthetics, using only paint. Richard Dean Anderson looks so young, that was hard work! For the final four stages (seventy, eighty, ninety and one hundred), prosthetic appliances were added, starting with the forehead. Jayne Dancose and Dave DuPuis were the special prosthetic visual effect artists and did an amazing job. It was quite a challenge," Newman adds, "but fortunately I'm allowed a certain amount of input, and one of the things that fascinates me about the ageing process is the way in which people's eyes change. It was very important to me that Richard Dean

Above: *Kynthia reminds O'Neill that he's never too old to learn.*

Anderson's eyes aged the way they should, and I was delighted when the lens technicians came up with a pair of very good contact lenses that really finished the job."

Newman also thought it was going to be a bit of a strain getting the actor, who's not normally associated with inactivity, to stay put for the length of time it took to apply the make-up. "Usually I can only pin Richard down for around seven minutes," Newman laughs, "but he was so intrigued by the whole old age procedure that it wasn't a problem at all. Taking the prosthetics off was the worst part. It took around two hours per day, and by that time Richard really was getting antsy!"

As on-set producer, Michael Greenburg acknowledges Anderson's professionalism during the filming of the episode: "It was very hard for Rick because of that make-up. He was being prepared for camera for anything between four and six hours every day. That has to be rough! But I also respect him for his incredible performance — from the piping voice to the stoop and shuffle. He did a wonderful job." λ

Thor's Hammer

Written by: Katharyn Powers	Guest cast: Gaylyn Gorg (Kendra), Vincent Hammond
Directed by: Brad Turner	(Unas), Tamsin Kelsey (Gairwyn), Mark Gibbon (Thor),
	James Earl Jones (the Voice of Unas)

On a peaceful mission to establish friendly relations with the people of Cimmeria, Teal'c and O'Neill are trapped by a mysterious bolt from the blue. They are transported to a strange underground labyrinth, from whence they must escape not only the caves but also the clutches of a very hungry, murderous creature called an Unas. In order to find and rescue their friends, Sam and Daniel must enlist the help of Kendra, a former Goa'uld host who escaped the labyrinth years before.

O'Neill on Thor's hologram

"I think we just got the answering machine."

"Episodes like this one are difficult shows to pull off and make 'real', for want of a better word in sci-fi," Michael Greenburg admits, "because ultimately it's actors and stunt men in suits. Fortunately, we found the very best special make-up effects people to help us." Speaking particularly of the Unas creature, Greenburg says, "Steve Johnson in LA did a great job. We had a ton of talented Vancouver people to help him out, but Steve is a real pro at making these alien suits look great. The way he applies the prosthetics to their faces really utilises the expressions of the actors. Remarkably, their skills shine through the rubber, and we can see the actors do all their little character nuances. Usually all you get is 'eyes', but with Steve doing the suits and prosthetics, you get all the acting talents of the performers coming through."

Producer John Smith, who joined the show with this episode,

The Unas

The ancient Egyptian king Unas was reputed to have hunted down and killed the gods by eating them. According to *Stargate SG-1* mythology, the Unas are a race of creatures whose looks inspire terror and who have a penchant for eating flesh — divine or otherwise. Once believed to be mere figments of Jaffa imagination (the Unas myth was used by parents to scare little Jaffa), they were thought to be the first creatures to be taken as hosts by the Goa'uld, and were employed as both slaves and taskmasters for the evil System Lords.

Above: The murderous Unas.

remembers being incredibly impressed by the talents of the prosthetic artist and cast: "They had a few problems getting it just right, but all credit to them for the great job they did." Although the Unas creature looks horrifying, Michael Greenburg reveals that all is not quite as it appears. "Since we made 'Thor's Hammer' we've been to the planet where they were conceived," he points out, "and met the Unas prior to their being taken over by the snakes. The Unas are actually good beings, very warm and friendly. They just look a little scary."

"You know," adds Greenburg, "when we destroyed the Goa'uld trap to allow Teal'c to escape in this episode, we literally left the door open for the Goa'uld to come back and haunt us. Which is exactly what happens much further along the way." λ

The Torment of Tantalus

Written by: Robert C. Cooper Directed by: Jonathan Glassner	Guest cast: Elizabeth Hoffman (Catherine Langford), Keene Curtis (Ernest Littlefield), Gary Jones (Technician), Duncan Fraser (Professor Langford), Nancy McClure (Young Catherine), Paul McGillion (Young Ernest)

Fascinated by archive footage showing a post-war team of boffins trying to unlock the secrets of the Stargate, Daniel Jackson makes a startling discovery. In 1945 a young professor, Ernest Littlefield, travelled through the wormhole, but a lack of information and technology left him stranded on the other side. SG-1 use the address to visit Ernest's destination, taking his former fiancée, Catherine Langford, along with them. They find the professor, now old, frail and suffering the effects of fifty years of solitary isolation, and discover a remarkable room that holds the combined wisdom of four alien civilisations. But the group must try to repair the damaged dial home device and return to Earth before the structure they are in disintegrates, and crashes into the sea hundreds of feet below.

Daniel to Jack

"The Pentagon said this was everything."

"Oh Please! The Pentagon's lost entire countries."

"I remember there were some truly major visual effects created for this episode," recalls producer John Smith. "They had the big castle, the big hole and the chamber with all the 'meaning of life' stuff. It looked fantastic. It was a very big episode, with lots of rain shots that had to be manufactured, which is pretty funny given the type of weather we have here in Vancouver!" One of the most amusing aspects for the producer was the way in which the cast and crew pulled together when the director suffered a minor memory slip. "This is probably slanderous and I apologise Mario," he grins, "but Mario Azzopardi simply forgot what he was meant to be filming. He looked at the call sheet and realised we had everybody there ready to shoot, but of course he hadn't had time to prepare. Being the genius he is, he just prepped it then and there, got on with it and pulled off some of the best scenes in the entire series. That's the nature of his talent."

"The floating doodads (very technical term) which made up 'the meaning of life stuff' in Ernest's chamber was a really good job," comments visual effects supervisor James Tichenor. But, modest to the last

he insists, "I ended up getting the full credit, but it was actually done with John Gajdecki and the guys from North West Imaging. What we were trying to do in that whole floating sequence was to come up with a way to represent a language in three dimensions. Most language is written on paper or in stone, so we wanted to represent some ideas in 3D. The tricky thing was getting a sense of depth, while still making sure the symbols were readable in such a big space. It took quite a lot of work to make things that were further away appear a little clearer, but when you do that, it kind of wrecks the depth. It was like two steps forward and one step back for us, because everything we did to make it easier for the person in the room to read the symbols actually worked against us in the shot. Still, it was a very pretty set!" ⋏

Above: O'Neill, about to reveal the secrets of the universe as Ernest Littlefield and Daniel stand by.

Bloodlines

Story by: Mark Saraceni	Guest cast: Tony Amendola (Bra'tac), Teryl Rothery
Teleplay by: Jeff King	(Dr Fraiser), Salli Richardson (Drey-Auc), Neil Denis
Directed by: Mario Azzopardi	(Rya'c)

D espite considerable risk, Teal'c returns to his home planet of Chulak in order to prevent his son Rya'c from becoming host to an infant Goa'uld, and thus a slave to Apophis. Aided by Bra'tac, Teal'c's 130 year-old Jaffa mentor, the team locate the ghetto where the family are thought to reside in time to stop the implantation ceremony. However, the wrath of the gods is nothing compared to the wrath of Teal'c's wife after he disrupts proceedings, killing the larva which would have saved his ailing child's life. Prepared to make the ultimate sacrifice by giving up his own larva to save his son, the Jaffa is restored when Sam and Daniel arrive bearing an unexpected gift.

O'Neill to Bra'tac

"Hey! Hey! Hey! Who are you calling a hassock?"

"'Bloodlines' is one of my all time favourites because it's where we gain some insight into Teal'c's deeper, more vulnerable side," begins Christopher Judge. "Until then, we mostly see him as kind of a stoic, a person who doesn't show much emotion. It's not that Teal'c's not emotional. It's that he has so *much* emotion that if everything that's boiling on the inside was to bubble to the surface, he would lose control. I have three kids of my own, so I could really relate to the character's dilemma

The Jaffa

A race of warriors, trained to protect the marauding parasites known as the Goa'uld. Denoted by the distinctive gold tattoo across their foreheads, they subjugate Goa'uld victims taken as slaves or 'hosts'. Before reaching puberty, Jaffa males receive their first larva during a ceremony known as the Prim'ta, when the creature is placed inside a specially cut pouch to incubate. The infant Goa'uld soon infects the entire body, taking over the immune system and almost completely depressing the personality of the 'host'. After approximately ten years, a new body is chosen by the mature symbiote and the Jaffa's military training can begin. Usually extremely loyal to one System Lord, Jaffa undertake their physical and mental instruction under the tutelage of a single mentor.

Above: Teal'c with his son Rya'c.

of having returned to resolve some personal issues with his wife and son, only to leave them once more. It was a great episode for me," he continues, "in that we get to meet Teal'c's mentor Bra'tac and get an idea of where Teal'c gets his strength of will and character, and what it means to be a Jaffa warrior."

Judge also feels much of the passion behind the Jaffa's actions is hinted at in 'Bloodlines'. "His objective in the episode is to prevent his son from becoming a slave to Apophis, but it also indicates that Teal'c's super-objective is to free all Jaffa from the slavery of the Goa'ulds. I see the likes of Bra'tac and Teal'c as the civil rights leaders of their time. In spite of the great sacrifice he has to make, Teal'c takes the chance to be free, and to free his people from the oppressors. From what I've gathered when speaking to guys who watch the show, most people see him the same way as I do, which is heroic and noble." λ

Fire and Water

Story by: Brad Wright
Teleplay by: Katharyn Powers
Directed by: Allan Eastman

Guest cast: Gerard Plunkett (Nem), Teryl Rothery (Dr Fraiser), Gary Jones (Technician)

SG-1 return from the planet Oannes without Daniel, who they last saw being engulfed in flames. But Jackson is being held in an underwater prison by Nem, an amphibious being, who believes the archaeologist can shed some light on the fate of Omoroca — the creature's partner who lived on Earth some 4,000 years ago. As Daniel struggles to assist his unlikely new friend, scouring his memory for pertinent facts from Babylonian history and agreeing to a potentially life-threatening scan of his brain, the rest of the SG-1 team are trying to come to terms with his death. Disturbed by dreams that suggest Daniel is still in the land of the living, the team resort to hypnosis to revisit the events leading up to his disappearance, and ultimately return to Oannes hoping to either rescue their colleague or lay his ghost to rest.

Daniel

"I would rather die than stay here in the knowledge that I would never see my wife or my friends again."

"The thing I loved most was that 'Fire and Water' had an entire emotional arc going on for me," says Michael Shanks. "As an actor, those kinds of things are always going to be fun to play. Opportunities like that are few and far between in *Stargate* because it's mostly about our reactions to what we see, rather than what we're put through. This was one of the strongest experiences I had within the course of the first season. One of the things I remember thinking about very clearly is that, actor-wise, you take a huge risk when you do that kind of episode. You put yourself right 'out there'. You're talking to a guy in a prosthetic suit, trying to reason with him; the context we're talking about is so crazily broad it can be disconcerting. It's potentially very embarrassing to go in on the day and say to some guy in a rubber suit, 'What are we talking about and what are you emoting about?' It's so crazily fictitious."

Speaking of his performance Shanks says, "It was just one of those things where I was young and naïve, and I think eager enough to completely throw myself into it, and commit to the wackiness entirely. Fortunately Gerard Plunkett, who played Nem, was great

Above: Daniel and Nem forging a friendship.

and did so much through that suit. He's a fine, strong actor and the director Allan Eastman was also great to work with. He gave us free rein to do whatever we wanted. He only directed one episode of *Stargate* but my favourite director's cut was the one for that show. It was too long for them to keep everything in, but considering it was one of those shows that looked quite 'iffy' on the page, it turned out rather well."

"This was another risky episode in season one," Brad Wright confirms. "I knew Michael Shanks could deliver in this difficult role, but every time you put your antagonist in a rubber suit, you'd better hope the actor pulls it off. I thought Gerard Plunkett did a tremendous job as Nem. I also enjoyed the matte painting at the water's edge. The scene was shot at a beach in Vancouver, so before the horizon was replaced in post production with a gas giant, there were sailboats and skyscrapers." ⅄

Hathor

Story by: David Bennett Carren & J. Larry Carroll Teleplay by: Jonathan Glassner Directed by: Brad Turner	Guest cast: Teryl Rothery (Dr Fraiser), Suanne Braun (Hathor), Dave Hurtubise (Dr Kleinhouse), Amanda O'Leary (Dr Cole)

Super-bitch Hathor — a Goa'uld who has taken on the persona of an Egyptian goddess — awakes from a 2,000 year slumber in a seriously bad mood and kills the hapless archaeologists responsible for disturbing her rest. She then inveigles her way into the Stargate facility in Cheyenne Mountain and, using an irresistible blend of physical charm, illicit substances and iron will, manages to seduce all the men on the base, convincing them to assist in her plan for world domination. As Hathor acquires the necessary DNA from Daniel and prepares Jack as her First Prime, it's up to Carter and the other women on the base to fight back.

Daniel to Jack

"Hathor was the Egyptian goddess of fertility, inebriety and music."

"Sex, drugs, and rock and roll?"

"In a manner of speaking."

"I happened to be watching TV and saw that an archaeologist had found an intact crypt in Egypt where they thought there had never been one," reveals Jonathan Glassner. "I thought, 'God, what if a Goa'uld was still trapped inside a tomb?' I did a little research and found out that, according to ancient mythology, Ra married his mother. So, I kind of spun it off from there and, yes, she really was the goddess of sex, drugs, and rock and roll! In fact, the black widow legend is based loosely on her because she killed most of the men she had sex with. She was a nasty, nasty woman."

Whilst, according to Glassner, Suanne Braun, the South African actress who portrays Hathor, was a delight, filming one of her scenes

Hathor

Mother of all Pharaohs, Hathor was patron of alcoholic beverages, music and dance, love and pregnant women. She almost obliterated Mankind until a vast quantity of blood-coloured beer made her too drunk to continue. It's claimed she could charm even the mighty Ra out of his darkest moods by dancing naked round his throne.

was less so: "You know the scene where she is in the big bath tub and all those little baby Goa'ulds are supposed to be coming out of her? Well, we were in *hell*! We could not get that scene to work. We had near on 1,000 of those little latex wormy things and we dumped them into the tub, thinking that the churning water would make them slime all around her. Instead they just floated to the top and sat there with the water churning away underneath. It looked just like she was sitting in a tub full of rubber things, and there was nothing we could do about it. We tried attaching them to fishing line and having the crew off-camera try to move them about, we tried all sorts of bizarre ways to make them look alive — but nothing worked. Then the visual effects guys, gods that they are, moseyed on over and said, 'Hey, you want us to fix that for ya?' They cut out each of those stupid little rubber things in post production and computer-animated them! So it's all down to those guys that we got the little critters jumping in and out of the water." ⅄

Above: Hathor enjoying a bubbling bath.

Singularity

Written by: Robert C. Cooper
Directed by: Mario Azzopardi

Guest cast: Teryl Rothery (Dr Fraiser), Katie Stuart (Cassandra), Gary Jones (Technician), Kevin McNulty (Dr Warner)

When SG-1 visit planet P8X987 they find that the population has been wiped out by a strange disease — with the exception of one little girl. A deep bond develops between Sam Carter and the child, Cassandra, but heartache is in store when it is discovered that a metallic device growing inside the girl is actually a time bomb, set by the Goa'uld in an effort to destroy Earth. Carter is torn between her love for Cassandra and her duty to protect the peoples of this world.

Sam Carter

"You didn't think the Colonel had a telescope on his roof just to look at the neighbours, did you?"

Clearly an emotional episode for the actress, Amanda Tapping retains special memories of some very touching moments during filming. "When I was doing the whole crying scene in the elevator, the crew were just so silent on our set," she remembers. "I've never heard it that quiet. We were just about to go to lunch and, that day, they just took grace without even thinking about it. Someone just stood and said, 'Let's take grace' and we did. I was really touched by that."

Although not yet appointed as creative consultant for the show at that time, Peter DeLuise watched every episode and attests, "The director, Mario Azzopardi, is a very passionate, volatile Maltese man and you can really see his influence in the scene when Carter leaves Cassandra to blow up. It's obvious that she's quite, quite moved, particularly when she's kicking the crap out of the lift — that's one of the moments where you can see Mario's passion come through."

"The director kept coming up to me saying, 'OK, do it again. I need more'," Tapping agrees, "but I was bawling my eyes out already. I was in the darkest place, but he kept on and, finally, on the last take, with the cameras rolling he said, 'Amanda, you have left this little girl in this horrible place and you are an evil person. You have left her alone. You are horrible.' Well, I just thought, 'I don't need this, I've already got it figured out,' so I turned to him and I yelled, 'Shut up! Get out of here!' And he said, 'Good! Now we shoot!' Afterwards he came up and said, 'Hey I got you angry. It was good.' But I thought 'No, it wasn't.' I felt terrible!"

Above: O'Neill and Teal'c make a break for the Gate.

Nevertheless, the resulting scene is powerfully effective.

For teenage actress Katie Stuart, the episode was most memorable for the extremely gentle treatment she received from the cast. "Everyone was very kind and made me feel very special," she recalls, "particularly Richard Dean Anderson. He kept trying to make me laugh — and usually did. He's such a great guy. Amanda and Teryl were very sweet, they really did make me feel like part of their family and, professionally, watching them work, I learned so much from them." Stuart admits to having some trouble parting from one of the extra cast members. "The dog O'Neill gives my character at the end of the show was really, really cute. I did *not* want to give him back." ⋏

Cor-Ai

Written by: Tom J. Astle Directed by: Mario Azzopardi	Guest cast: Peter Williams (Apophis), David McNally (Hanno), Paulina Gillis (Byrsa Woman), Christina Jastrzembska (Member of the Council of Ancients), Michasa Armstrong (Shak'l)

The game is almost up for Teal'c when the SG-1 team visit P3X1279 — a world the Jaffa recognises as Chartago — home to a race called the Bysra. A favourite place for the Goa'uld to harvest hosts, one of the residents recognises Teal'c as Apophis's First Prime, promptly accuses him of murdering his father and demands the maximum penalty for such a crime. O'Neill and the rest of the team must use all the skills at their disposal to persuade Teal'c's accuser, the Council of Ancients and the Jaffa himself that the death sentence is not appropriate in this case.

O'Neill to Daniel

"Why does it always have to be a religious thing with you? Couldn't they just be coming from a swap meet?"

"This was such a cool episode to do," announces Christopher Judge. Apart from the fact that he had a bunch of women fawning all over him (in the scene where Teal'c's body is anointed before death), the deeper significance of the story has a strong appeal. "I get put on trial for a crime I allegedly did before I left the service of Apophis — I thought it was great of the writers to go down that track.

"I think the episode really cut to the quick of Teal'c's whole ideology," Judge continues. "And that is: 'You are ultimately responsible for your actions, and you have to be ready to face the consequences of those actions, no matter what position you later find yourself in.' There's a great line where Teal'c says, 'I'm sorry O'Neill. I will not run.' And to me that is the very core of Teal'c. He believes — 'I did this. Even though I was following orders and serving Apophis when I killed Hanno's father, I am still responsible for that man's death. The victims of that attack deserve retribution. They deserve to extract whatever revenge for my bad deed that they think is due to me. If I am a man, then I have to sit there and accept it.' It's a matter of honour and honesty above everything else, which to me describes exactly what Teal'c is about. I think the audience really got to see that, probably for the first time, in 'Cor-Ai'. The message to me was that, though anyone can change, you're still held accountable for your actions and

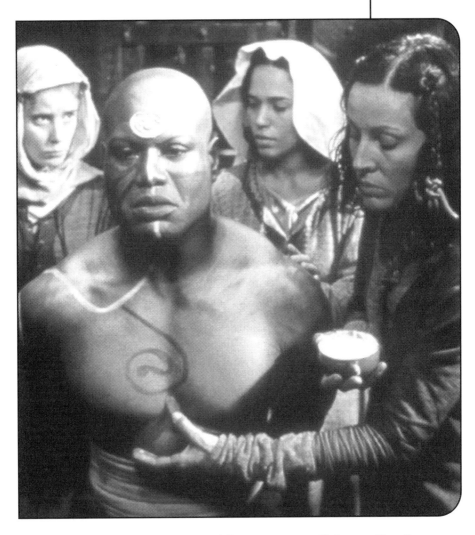

it's not enough just to say, 'Hey! I'm a different person now.'" On a personal note, the actor reveals, "That was something I was going through as a person at the time, so that episode really spoke to me."

In a lighter vein, Judge describes the filming of the story as being particularly pleasurable because "I get to take my shirt off! It's a common thread in all the episodes that I enjoy. I'm not sure what that means." He further admits, "I spent the scene where the women are preparing my body giggling my ass off. I've come to the conclusion that Teal'c was a nudist on Chulak!" ⋏

Above: Bysran Handmaids attend to Teal'c.

Enigma

Written by: Katharyn Powers	Guest cast: Tobin Bell (Omoc), Garwin Sanford (Narim),
Directed by: William Gereghty	Tom McBeath (Colonel Mayborne), Gerard Plunkett (Tuplo), Gary Jones (Technician), Frida Betrani (Lya)

Despite being rescued from certain death when a volcano threatens their lives, the Tollan are less than grateful for SG-1's efforts. The Tollan leader — a dour individual named Omoc — dismisses the Earth's population as primitive, refuses to share information about his planet's technology and demands to be sent to a world where their advanced knowledge can be appreciated. However, Narim — a far friendlier individual with more than a passing interest in the fair Samantha Carter — lets slip that Omoc's father once shared Tollan advancements with a civilisation very similar to Earth. The result was a civil war that destroyed the primitive planet and destabilised Tollan. With military intelligence threatening to force the Tollan to improve weapon systems, SG-1 must try to prevent a similar disaster from occuring.

Carter to O'Neill

"Air — in pockets from 1500 down to 200 degrees."

"Sounds like LA."

"'Enigma' was an interesting episode because it introduced the Tollan to us," says Brad Wright. Acknowledging that they were a pretty miserable bunch, he continues, "They have become the allies who won't give us anything. This story was when we looked the Prime Directive [*Star Trek*'s famous 'non-interference' law] in the face, except *we* were the ones who failed to benefit from the Tollan Prime Directive! The Tollan had the Prime Directive, and we were pissed

The Tollan

A highly advanced race, the Tollan are on a par with the alliance of super beings that protect all that is good in the universe. Whilst their superior technology could assist the humans on Earth to develop a weapon to defend against Goa'uld attack, the Tollan do not consider us intellectually or morally developed enough to use it for defence purposes only, and refuse to share their knowledge. Rescued by SG-1 and aided by the Nox, the Tollan are relocated to a new home world. Their special powers include walking through walls, telepathy and extra sensory perception.

off by that. I mean, we had saved them from death by volcano!" Hinting at some appearances in later seasons, Wright confirms, "We did make a good friend in Narim. I think it's great that a character like his can come back over the course of the show, which is a significant amount of time, and renew their acquaintance with us. To the general audience he may be just a guy, but for the fans it helps them recognise that we have a bit of a 'fabric' going. A fan actually described what we're trying to do here by writing on the internet, '*Stargate SG-1* may not be the best show on television, but it is something of a rather meaty novel. It's a novel that has got hundreds and hundreds of chapters but remembers where the book began.' *Stargate* has had the continuity of myself and Robert Cooper making sure that characters like Narim come back, and that the Tollan are still the Tollan, as opposed to some other strange race, and I think all of us have benefited from that." λ

Above: A tender moment for Carter and Narim.

Solitudes

| Written by: Brad Wright | Guest cast: Gary Jones (Technician), Dan Shea |
| Directed by: Martin Wood | (Sergeant Siler) |

Things go from cold and frosty to hot and heavy when O'Neill and Carter are trapped in an icy wilderness after their trip through the Stargate goes badly wrong. Seriously injured with a broken leg and internal bleeding, O'Neill fights to stay alive whilst Carter struggles with the nearby Stargate, trying desperately to make it work. Back at Stargate Command, Teal'c and Daniel are working around the clock to try to decipher where in a million worlds their compatriots could be.

Carter to O'Neill

"Colonel?"

"It's my side arm, I swear. No giggling."

As far as Sam Carter's *alter ego* is concerned, the scene where she and O'Neill share body heat to keep warm was "a major coup for the writers who discovered their sense of humour, and brought it into that situation. It was not an ad-lib. That 'side arm' line was actually written in there." Amanda Tapping also recalls her own heroic efforts to lighten things up: "There is a scene at the DHD when O'Neill comes crawling up, his leg broken. It's a 'two-shot' of us with a 'close-up' on me, and director Martin Wood suggested that if I had a chance to have some fun with the shot to go for it, because it was freezing cold and we were all miserable. So Rick says, 'Can you dig it out?' and he is expecting me to reply something like, 'If we can't, we can use the chipped ice we melt for drinking water.' But I yelled, 'Can we dig it out? You spent seven years on *MacGyver* and you can't figure this out?' Rick's eyes got really big, but I just carried on saying, 'God! We've got a belt buckle, a shoelace, a stick of gum… build us a nuclear reactor for crying out loud! You used to be MacGadget, MacGimmick. Now you're just MacUseless,' and then wailed away about being stuck on a glacier with MacGyver. It was hilarious…

"I got to take an amazing helicopter ride with this renegade crew up to Pemberton Icefield, which is north of Whistler," Tapping continues. "They literally plonked me on this icefield, and then the helicopter flew up further away so they could shoot a long lens whilst I crawled into a crevasse and crawled out again. At the time I kept thinking, 'Ohmigod! I am never going to get the opportunity to do this again.'" Although awe-inspiring, the actress concedes that "it was freezing cold and I got really

Above: Comrades in arms.

wet, and then had a forty-five minute ride back in the helicopter, but I just remember thinking that I was so lucky." Lucky or not, Tapping insists it was scary too: "I was hiding in this crevasse with my arms sticking out, but I was perched on one foot on a tiny ice ledge, and could have slipped. Added to that I kept hearing these really loud booms so, using my radio, I spoke to the safety officer and asked what they were. 'Oh don't worry about it,' he said, 'It's just an avalanche.' It was seriously scary. You could hear the ice moaning and groaning — but what an experience, eh?" ⅄

Tin Man

| Written by: Jeff King | Guest cast: Teryl Rothery (Dr Fraiser), Jay Brazeau |
| Directed by: Jimmy Kaufman | (Harlan) |

Rendered unconscious by an electrical trap on PX3989, SG-1 awake to find that Harlan, an elderly native of the planet (he claims to be 11,000 years old) has repaired and improved their damaged bodies. On their return to the Stargate Command Centre, the team discovers that all is not as it seems — their human bodies have been replaced by machines. Needless to say, SG-1 are less than impressed with their robot selves and return to the planet to demand that normal service be resumed as soon as possible. Hoping a compromise can be achieved between the machine shop team and the human originals, the well-meaning Harlan introduces SG-1 to 'themselves', with hilarious but also touching results.

O'Neill

> "What, this is better — I'm dead?"

"This was such a fun episode to do," says Michael Greenburg. "Jay Brazeau is a brilliant actor and can really use a comic beat. Production-wise the episode was quite difficult, because we were shooting in an old abandoned power station that was tricky to light and work in. On top of that, we were doing a ton of 'twinning' shots, which involved split screens, motion control and tracking shots. It certainly was one of those episodes that really tests your film-making abilities."

"Jon Glassner and I were flying back from LA," recalls Brad Wright, "and we had to solve a problem, because the story had evolved where Jeff King wanted to turn the team into robots, but we didn't know how to end it. Then I came up with the idea that they find their bodies. The whole notion that we were trying to solve through the episode was, 'How do we get back into our bodies?' That's what an audience is going to ask. Now Harlan says it's impossible, but the reason for that is because the bodies are occupied. The brainstorm I had was that SG-1 hadn't been *transferred* into the robots — they had been *copied*. I thought it was really cool that we weren't even following 'our' characters through the episode, but one hundred per cent copies of them instead."

One of the Wright's favourite scenes is when O'Neill leaves O'Neill: "Rick really enjoyed the challenge of predicting his own

rhythms, and imagining what it was like to respond to himself. Don't forget he would do one side, then the camera was locked off, and he would change costume and go do the other side. There were hours and hours in between but he had to respond as if it had just happened."

Above: Teal'c shows Harlan he is less than pleased.

"The episode has a big place in my heart because it was the first time we'd gone for out-and-out comedy," Wright adds. "Before 'Tin Man' we were allowing the humour to come through, but within a serious story. This was the first time we let a guest character be balls-out funny." Clearly a fan of the actor, Wright grins, "Jay Brazeau is a local Vancouver actor and I wrote Harlan for him. That was why there were all those funny little moments, like when he'd say 'You're different!' I knew exactly how he'd deliver that."

For Wright, the idea of re-visiting the alternative SG-1 team is an extremely tempting possibility: "They are still out there, you know…" ⅄

There But For the Grace of God

Story by: David Kemper	Guest cast: Elizabeth Hoffman (Catherine Langford),
Teleplay by: Robert C. Cooper	Gary Jones (Technician), Stuart O'Connell (Marine),
Directed by: David Warry-Smith	Michael Kopsa (News Anchor)

The inquisitive Daniel Jackson accidentally activates the doorway to an alternative universe during an exploratory mission to P3R233. Emerging through the Stargate into what looks like home, the archaeologist steps into a world where things are not as familiar as they seem. Earth is under attack by Goa'uld forces that have already killed half a billion people, and are about to capture Stargate Command.

Teal'c is still First Prime to Apophis and there's more than just a working relationship between Sam Carter and O'Neill. Unable to prevent the total annihilation of the peoples of this world, Daniel must find a way to get back to his own reality to prevent the same thing happening there.

Daniel Jackson

"Unless the last two years have been a wacky, wacky dream I am a member of SG-1."

Things may have seemed like a wacky dream to the team's archaeologist, but for Amanda Tapping this episode was more a dream come true. "I remember getting to have hair!" she laughs. On a more serious note, the actress confides that the farewell scene between the alternative O'Neill and Carter was actually written as a kiss, but says, "Both of us looked at each other and said, 'Let's make it a hug.'" Working on the basis that 'less is more', Tapping suggests, "I actually think the hug was much better than a kiss — to me it conveyed a much deeper level of feeling." Of her co-star she says, "I am so glad we were both on the same page with it. It's not that I didn't want to kiss Richard Dean Anderson — I did want to! Just don't tell anybody."

One man bursting to tell everybody about the episode is Gary Jones who, as the Technician, is usually well and truly behind the screens, if not the scenes, at Stargate Command. "My character got to fire a machine gun in this episode," he beams. Admitting that it was "cool, but scary", Jones recounts, "One of the crew handed me a fully automatic weapon and asked if I'd fired one before. I said, 'Wow, are you kidding? No!' So we went out to the parking lot, he handed me a pair of ear defenders, put a blank clip in the gun and told me to fire away. I couldn't hear a thing, but there were sparks flying out from the side of the gun! When we were ready to shoot the scene I stood between Don Davis and

three huge stunt men. The sound, when we started firing, was unbelievable. That's one of the reasons why I love coming on the show — you never know quite what you're in for when you turn up for work."

Given that these kinds of episodes can be a trifle risky, Robert Cooper (who wrote the teleplay from a story by David Kemper, now best known as executive producer of *Farscape*) is quietly proud of the result. "'There But For the Grace of God' is an example of an alternative reality which worked quite well," he says modestly. λ

Above: A distraught Daniel watches an Earth's demise.

Politics

Written by: Brad Wright	Guest cast: Ronny Cox (Senator Kinsey), Robert
Directed by: Martin Wood	Wisden (Lieutenant Colonel Samuels)

Following his return from an alternative Earth, Daniel Jackson is determined that the information he obtained there be used to prevent cataclysmic disaster on our planet. However, whilst the Goa'uld stalk towards this Earth reality, the SG-1 team must deal with a far more immediate danger to the Stargate. The powerful chairman of the Appropriations Committee has decided that the Stargate project is not worth the billions of tax dollars spent on it each year, and wants to bury the Gate and close the programme. Even though Daniel insists that the Gate is the only way to help save the world, his words hold no sway with the men in suits.

O'Neill to Carter

"Engaged?"

"Theoretically it's possible."

"It's against regulations."

Brad Wright admits that 'Politics' was "unashamedly a clip show, which almost always happens in the first season of a show that does a pilot as big as we did. The episode was designed to save money. I have done several clip shows (which is not something I'm particularly proud of) but one of the things I've learned when doing them is to get a star — and we had a great one in Ronny Cox." Cox is totally convincing as Senator Kinsey, the impartial voice of reason supposedly protecting the American people's hard earned dollar. It's just one in a long line of memorable performances: Cox's film credits include *RoboCop*, *Total Recall* and *Deliverance*, and television appearances include *LA Law* and *Star Trek: The Next Generation*. So, as well as having a great guest star, Wright then insists the only way forward is to "create a story that stands alone even if you don't see the clips."

"Before we put the clips in," Wright explains, "I edited the show and made a tight little episode. Granted it was only 26 minutes long so the remainder needed to be clips, but I knew what the clips were going to be, because obviously I had set up the examples within the story. The goal was to create a good dynamic. The other rule I have is that I don't have a clip in the pre-credits 'tease', act one, or act five, so the audience doesn't know it's a clip show until they are fully on board."

Above: Senator Kinsey displays US tax dollars at work.

Honest in his assessment of the episode, Wright confirms, "Some people don't feel that episode is very good. They feel a little bit ripped off. With clip shows, fans are seeing things they've already seen before, but the person who has never watched the show before — they don't mind that at all. But what I tried to do, and what I think Ronny delivered very nicely, was a really good performance leading to a cliffhanger. It was also the beginning of Ronny's participation in *Stargate SG-1*. He's been back several times in the course of the show, and it's great for us to have a recurring character of his calibre."

Wright was also delighted to welcome Martin Wood as director for the first time: "He did a very good job, that's the reason we brought him back time and time again." λ

Within the Serpent's Grasp

Story by: James Crocker **Teleplay by:** Jonathan Glassner **Directed by:** David Warry-Smith	**Guest cast:** Peter Williams (Apophis), Gary Jones (Technician), Alexis Cruz (Skaara/Klorel), Brent Stait (Major Ferretti)

T hings are not going well. The Stargate programme is being shut down by the US Government, just as the Goa'uld — as Daniel had predicted — decide to stake their claim to Earth. The SG-1 team make an unauthorised trip through the Stargate to try to slow down or prevent the attack, and find themselves on an enemy ship full of Jaffa warriors. To make matters worse, they discover that the Stargate is no longer able to dial home to Earth. The team is left with no choice but to wire the ship with the explosives they brought with them, and go down fighting. But while Carter and Jackson set as many explosives as they can around the ship, O'Neill and Teal'c see Skaara, once O'Neill's Abydonian friend, but now the host to Klorel, Apophis's son. They quickly realise that their only hope of escape is the slim possibility that Skaara's strength of spirit will enable him to temporarily conquer the Goa'uld that inhabits his body, and help SG-1 save the day.

O'Neill

"I always get a happy, tingly feeling when I see those guys."

Both Brad Wright and Jonathan Glassner are happy to confess that the fans of the show were responsible for a major change of plan. "As far as we were concerned the Skaara character was dead," begins Glassner. "We'd hinted that we were going to kill him, and we actually did... " Brad Wright continues, "But we'd started getting the message from fans that he was a really popular character and we thought, 'Boy, if we kill him, they are going to kill us!'" Glassner goes on, "In fact, when news of the character's death leaked out, the fans went ballistic. They were furious. We didn't think they would care that much, but the volume of mail convinced us Skaara had to stay. So, thanks to the visual effects guys, we digitally cut him out of a previous scene and pasted him into one that was supposedly after he would have been dead, to show that he was alive and was going to get away. Toward the end of the episode, when Apophis makes his escape, it looks as though Klorel/Skaara is standing behind him in the rings that will whisk him to safety — but he wasn't there originally! Thank God we didn't kill him off, because we went on to do a bunch of great episodes with Alexis."

A firm favourite with the fans, Richard Dean Anderson adds his approval of the episode, saying, "It was really cool. We used the Gate, we were out in space, it had bad guys, good guys and a cliffhanger. I loved it."

Above: Teal'c and O'Neill coming up on Earth.

"A large-scale miniature of Apophis's ship was built for the pull out shot from inside the command centre in 'Within the Serpent's Grasp'," reveals special effects supervisor John Gajdecki. "Then for the close up, we constructed a very large model — which was actually twenty feet across at the base — shot it with motion control and composited that into a starfield with a computer generated mothership in the background." All in all, the episode made a stunning end to *Stargate SG-1*'s début season. ʎ

Serpent's Lair

Written by: Brad Wright	Guest cast: Peter Williams (Apophis), Tony Amendola
Directed by: Jonathan Glassner	(Bra'tac), Gary Jones (Technician), Alexis Cruz
	(Skaara/Klorel), Robert Wisden (Lieutenant Colonel
	Samuels)

With Earth facing total annihilation from a fleet of Goa'uld warships, it is left to those at Stargate Command to devise and carry out counter measures to try and avoid the destruction of the human race. As a precaution, America's top scientists and politicians are sent through the Gate to off-world safety, whilst SG-1 use the device to embark on a daring mission of their own. Inadvertently boarding one of the incoming ships, which is being commanded by Klorel, adopted son of Apophis, the team find themselves facing a dilemma where the only solution is to blow up the ship, and hence themselves, to save the planet.

O'Neill

"Call me a pessimist, but I think it's time for a new plan."

"Remember the scene where O'Neill and Bra'tac are getting ready to blast off in the glider?" asks Tony Amendola. "Well, to shoot that they had us on a platform, about twelve feet off the ground, and because we were supposed to be blasted out into space, they had to secure the hatch above us. They had to do it, not just for dramatic purposes but in a practical sense too, because there was going to be turbulence, and we had a big wind machine blowing sand in our faces, so they put this glass top over us. Then they screwed it shut, so you can imagine it got a little claustrophobic. Added to that, we're sitting there quietly wondering when there would be time to go to the bathroom!

"Of course, the assistant director always assures you that it's only

Death Gliders

The Goa'uld Death Gliders are small, swift flying machines able to carry one to two persons. Resembling a flying insect or bat, these deadly fighting craft are armed with laser weapons capable of pinpoint accuracy. Huge banks of Death Gliders are stored in enormous stellar hangers inside Goa'uld motherships, ready for the highly trained Jaffa who pilot them.

Above: A Death Glider escapes an exploding Goa'uld mothership.

going to be a twenty-minute thing. Two hours and twenty minutes later we were *still* sitting there, but it was great because I thought, 'Whatever I'm going through, I know that one of the producers is sitting right next to me, going through it too. It was a great bonding experience for Richard Dean Anderson and I. We sang songs and had a little chat. Richard made me feel really at home there."

Visual effects supervisor John Gajdecki reveals how the spectacular scene with the SG-1 team slipping from the Serpent's Lair was achieved: "Death Glider models were built for that final sequence as our heroes escape from the exploding Goa'uld motherships. Each model was approximately two and a half feet in wing span, and these miniatures were shot against a green screen using motion control techniques. Subtle camera moves and reflections were added in post production to make the shots seemingly and seamlessly match the surrounding footage." ⋋

In the Line of Duty

Written by: Robert C. Cooper
Directed by: Martin Wood

Guest cast: Teryl Rothery (Dr Fraiser), Katie Stuart (Cassandra), Judy Norton (Talia), Peter Lacroix (Ashrak)

Whilst on a rescue mission to the planet Nasya, which had been attacked by the Gao'uld, Samantha Carter's fate seems sealed with a kiss, when her body is invaded by a Goa'uld symbiote as she administers first aid to a wounded local. Unbeknown to the rest of the team, she brings the alien back to Earth, where even a medical check fails to notice the change. Only Cassandra, who has Naquadah in her blood, can sense the Goa'uld within her adopted mother. Captured and imprisoned, during negotiations for Carter's life, the Goa'uld finally reveals its identity as Jolinar of Malkshur, a member of a rebel Goa'uld group known as the Tok'ra, who oppose the system lords' practice of subduing other races. It also announces that an assassin specially trained to kill Goa'uld by the name of Ashrak is hunting it, and will not hesitate to kill Carter to get to Jolinar unless stopped by SG-1.

> **Teal'c**
>
> "When you speak to her, do not see your friend."

It may have started off as a cost-cutting exercise, but 'In the Line of Duty' ended up being one of the pivotal episodes of *Stargate SG-1*. Jonathan Glassner explains: "When we originally came up with the idea, it was for it to be what we call a 'bottle show', which means it's all made 'inside the bottle', just using our regular sets so we don't need to build new ones. On bottle shows we use our regular cast and often we don't have to cast any new actors. It's much less expensive to produce, and is done to make up costs when we've gone over budget making other episodes. But then we proceeded to shoot the 'teaser', which — much to the chagrin of the studio — was expensive, because of all the attacks and fly-pasts and extra cast members. So we ended up coming in on budget rather than under budget. I guess we strayed from the original purpose of saving money, but we just had too much fun making the teaser to cut back on anything else!

"The thing about the episode which is important for the series is that it's when we first mention the Tok'ra. It's funny how things develop. The Tok'ra came out of a need in that particular episode to give us a moral and ethical ambiguity on what to do about the Goa'uld

Above: Saving Captain Carter.

that had taken over Sam Carter, but introducing the Tok'ra basically changed the whole series."

"I found that really hard," Amanda Tapping volunteers. "I just remember stillness and being really dark. I was in a very dark place, and it was particularly difficult to do the scene where Sam first comes into the Gateroom raging because I'd never played and never shown that type of anger with Carter. The tossing O'Neill aside part was a lot of fun, but for the most part it was very difficult. Michael, Christopher and Richard were trying to make me laugh in the darkest scene, because each of them had an individual moment with me and they tried to lighten it for me. I just remember trying to get a different physicality for her." ⋏

Prisoners

Written by: Terry Curtis Fox
Directed by: David Warry-Smith

Guest cast: Bonnie Bartlett (Linea), Colin Lawrence (Major Warren), Andrew Whekler (Major Stan Kovacek), Mark Acheson (Vishnor), Michael Puttonen (Simian), Colleen Winton (Dr Greene)

The SG-1 team discover that 'one good turn' does not necessarily bring the expected reward. After helping a man who turns out to be a fleeing murderer, the team are condemned to spend the rest of their days in a penal colony. Populated by a mismatch of brutish characters where survival of the fittest is the order of the day, SG-1 are surprised to find the place ruled by a frail-looking woman called Linea. Working together, SG-1 and Linea devise a plan for escape and manage to make it back to Earth. But events come full circle as the 'one good turn' motto is put to the test once more, with unexpected and frightening results.

Linea

"There are many forms of power, my dear, some more subtle than others."

"Smoking shoes, gruel out of a trough, big, tough, hairy guys — yeah, I remember that one," grins John Smith. "It was a really dark and grimy set but everyone had fun. Rick has a great sense of humour so there were a lot of heehaws that week." Amanda Tapping laughs, "It was all about dirt! That whole episode was dirty. In 'Prisoners' we had all these amazing extras. The background performers were really big, freaky looking guys. Walking into that set, it was dirty and dark and smelly, and we were surrounded by these scary looking guys. It was cool!"

It might have been a blast, but it was also a major pain in the butt for the producers of the show. "We had a problem when we built that whole underground, dark, dirty set on the sound stage because it ended up taking around three or four weeks to get all of that dirt out of everything!" explains Jonathan Glassner. "It got in the lights, it got in the machinery, the whole place was filthy. We used dry dirt, when we should have used mud, so it would stick to stuff. Because it was dust, every time anyone took a step, it would kick up clouds of it everywhere. We actually built that set on one of our back-up sound stages," he continues. "The ceiling in there was too low for our Stargate to fit properly. We don't usually build sets and have a Stargate on them, so our Gate had to be put on an angle so it was leaning over. That's the only way we could get it to fit."

Above: SG-1 *receive judgement from above.*

"'Prisoners' was an opportunity to show that our guys don't always get it right," Glassner suggests. "With one character in particular, our people screwed up and let her get away, and she will show up again in some form or other. But in order to keep the mystery, we didn't want to be unrealistic, and have the team find her in the next episode, because if she can hide from every species including the Goa'uld, she can outwit our guys for a time. She got away with some pretty nasty stuff, but we will find her!" ʎ

The Gamekeeper

Story by: Jonathan Glassner & Brad Wright
Teleplay by: Jonathan Glassner
Directed by: Martin Wood

Guest cast: Dwight Shultz (The Keeper), Teryl Rothery (Dr Fraiser), Jay Acovone (Kawalsky), Michael Rogers (Colonel John Michaels), Lisa Bunting (Claire Jackson), Robert Duncan (Melburn Jackson)

The SG-1 team travel to a "fertile garden world" known as P7J989, and promptly find themselves the wrong side of Paradise. Trapped inside strange metallic chambers, they wake up to a 'virtual' reality controlled by the mysterious Keeper, who forces the team to relive painful moments from their lives over and over again. What's more, the attempts by Daniel and O'Neill to alter the outcome of their experiences are being used to entertain the other "residents" of the planet, who are being misled by the Keeper. Under the pretence that the world outside has been made uninhabitable by pollution, he has kept them "under wraps" for over a thousand years. SG-1 must find a way to free the residents and themselves before past memories drive them insane...

The Keeper

> "I am the Keeper of all that is, was and will be."

Jonathan Glassner is very pleased with the way this episode turned out: "'The Gamekeeper' came out of an idea we had way back when we were developing the stories. All the writers were sitting in a room, and we didn't think we had explored some of the characters' pasts enough. We hadn't expanded on their back stories enough for the audience to get to know them, and we pondered how to do that without either going back in time, or having them sit around talking about it! Eventually we came up with the concept of a video game scenario, which gave us a way of exploring the death of Daniel Jackson's parents in sort of a sci-fi way." Michael Shanks says, "It went some way to showing why Daniel is the way he is, and it was a challenge to make it all make sense." On set producer Michael Greenburg adds, "The idea of being in a game situation was really cool, and Dwight Shultz did a tremendous job as the Keeper."

"There's this big Dome in Vancouver — the Observatory in Queen Elizabeth Park," Glassner continues. "It's basically a really big greenhouse. It's a botanical garden, and surrounding it outside are all these other pristine, beautiful gardens. It's a favourite with tourists, and when anyone came to visit me in Vancouver I would take them there for Saturday brunch.

One time I was there it suddenly came to me — we had to use it as a set! We didn't think we could get it, because it's very protected; the ecosystem is very delicate and fragile. But I wrote the episode as if we were going to film there, and then actually persuaded them to go for it. It turned out that one of the people in charge was a huge fan of the show and he said, 'Sure! Just don't touch any of the plants.'" Glassner is keen to point out that all of the plants the cast *do* touch in the episode were put there by the production designers and crew! ⋏

Above: Teal'c instructs the Gamekeeper in the error of his ways.

Need

Written by: Robert C. Cooper & Damian Kindler	Guest cast: Teryl Rothery (Dr Fraiser), Heather Hanson (Shyla), George Touliatos (Pyrus)
Directed by: Robert C. Cooper	

O n the planet P3R636, Daniel Jackson comes to the aid of a beautiful princess as she attempts to throw herself from a cliff-top. Rather than being heralded as a hero, he and the rest of the team are imprisoned by her irate father and set to work in Naquadah mines. After sustaining serious injury whilst trying to escape, Daniel is looked after by the Princess, who uses a Goa'uld sarcophagus to restore his health. While the pair take their relationship further, his team-mates are left to suffer in the mines. As Daniel learns the secrets of the planet, he also tries to secure the freedom of the rest of SG-1, but an irresistible temptation could scupper all their plans.

> **Sam to O'Neill**
>
> "Lately I get this weird feeling when I'm near Teal'c."
>
> "Who doesn't?"

"This was another dirty episode," grins Amanda Tapping. "Rick already had make-up dirt on him, but then he'd go round and pick up dirt from the floor and wipe it all over himself, and anyone else nearby. We were all filthy. I remember going home and washing my hair and laughing at the colour of the water in the sink. It was great fun though. I love getting dirty better than getting pretty!"

Renowned for really getting into his role, Michael Shanks reacts to

The Sarcophagus

A seriously essential tool for a Goa'uld or anyone else seeking near eternal life, the Sarcophagus is a transportable rejuvenating/healing machine. No less stunning in impact than the Nox 'Ritual of Life', this mechanical life-saving device has been used by the Goa'uld and other races to keep body and soul together for thousands of years. However, as with all karma-ceutical products, repeated use can cause addictive behaviour in humans. Withdrawal from the short-term benefits of the sarcophagus can cause normally docile individuals to fidget, shout, scream and throw punches at doctors, best friends or anyone else who stands in their way. Attempts by humans in ancient Egypt to copy sarcophagus technology were woefully inadequate, with occupants ending up mummified instead of reborn.

*Above: Daniel bids
Shyla a fond farewell.*

the compliment that he played the part of an addict with considerable aplomb. Laughing, he insists, "I'm not going to comment on that," before going on to shrug "it was one of those things. It was early on in the second season and is another one of those episodes where I look back and think 'Ohmigod! I was terrible in that.'

"It's tough to fully comment on the episode," Shanks continues, "because there is so much objectivity between those days and now. What happens is, I'm apt to think about how I would have played a particular scene in a different way to improve on the performance I gave, which is what I tend to do with a lot of my work. Looking back though, I think there were some nice moments. 'Need' was a good character episode."

Shanks also feels the story was one of the strongest to highlight the bond between Jack O'Neill and his team. "The scene toward the end, where O'Neill puts his life on the line to support Daniel physically and mentally," he notes, "shows how far their friendship has evolved from the days when O'Neill just thought of Daniel as a geek." ⅄

Thor's Chariot

Written by: Katharyn Powers	Guest cast: Tamsin Kelsey (Gairwyn), Andrew Kavadas
Directed by: William Gereghty	(Olaf), Douglas H. Arthurs (Heru-ur), Mark Gibbon (Thor)

Returning to Cimmeria, which is now under attack from the Goa'uld, SG-1 meet up with Gairwyn, whom they met on their first trip to the planet, and her friend Olaf. It was on this initial visit that the team destroyed Thor's Hammer, the planet's only defence against the Goa'uld. Though Carter accidentally discovers that she can use the Goa'uld ribbon device, the team know that they are going to need all the help they can get to defeat the massive enemy force led by the system lord Heru-ur. Whilst O'Neill and Teal'c head off on a scouting mission only to find themselves confronting the enemy head-on, Carter, Jackson and Gairwyn return to the Hall of Thor's Might hoping to find other weapons. Instead, the trio find themselves facing a series of tests set by a hologram of Thor, the Asgard god who supposedly guards the planet. The race is on — can they solve the riddles in the runes, and what, if anything, will happen if they do? With time running out, it looks as if Heru-ur will succeed in leading his invading army to victory…

Daniel Jackson

"I don't suppose this is the best time to bring up my problem with heights?"

Visual effects supervisor James Tichenor is understandably proud of the effects in 'Thor's Chariot', saying, "I really liked the floor drop-

Thor

Small, slim, with huge friendly eyes and a soft spot for Samantha Carter, Thor is leader of the Asgard, one of the four races sworn to protect the galaxies. Although too advanced to be concerned about his true personal appearance, Thor and other members of his kind often use holographic imagery to appear as larger-than-life gods and warriors from Earth's Nordic past. A mutual partnership of respect and trust has grown between the Asgard and the people of Earth since Thor removed the threat of certain death from SG-1 by arriving in his ship and zapping a gang of Goa'uld henchmen. The SG team repaid the debt by rescuing the little grey man from a battalion of nasty mechanical beasts that were trying to eat him out of house and home. It's intriguing to note that Thor, the Norse God of Thunder's greatest enemy is Jormungard — the Midgard Serpent. Remind you of anyone?

Above: Solving riddles — Asgard style.

away shot, which was done in conjunction with Rainmaker Digital Pictures. It was one of those things where we were wondering whether or not we could do it, because it was such a dynamic simulation, and is something that we would generally shoot using a model. Being a TV show with a TV budget meant that was out of the question, so we simulated it all in CG. The pit was a matte painting that was done by Kent Matheson. When Gairwyn was walking along the beam and we were looking down on her, she was actually only five inches off the ground! We had green screen on either side of her, painted all of that away and put the pit in. The angles where we're looking from the pit up to her, we put the platform up about six feet, so you get the idea that she could fall off the beam."

Recalling the trepidation he felt at the start of the episode, Tichenor smiles when he remembers the result: "When we showed it to Jonathan Glassner, who had been warned the effect was so difficult to achieve he might not get quite what he expected, he took one look at it, said, 'Great!' and moved on. That felt really good." ᛟ

Message in a Bottle

Story by: Michael Greenburg & Jarrad Paul Teleplay by: Brad Wright Directed by: David Warry-Smith	Guest cast: Teryl Rothery (Dr Fraiser), Tobias Mehler (Lieutenant Graham Simmons), Gary Jones (Technician), Dan Shea (Sergeant Siler), Kevin Conway (SG Leader)

lien technology tends to be unpredictable, as the team discover when they bring an orb back through the Stargate. During tests to try and determine its self-sufficient power source, the orb seems to destabilise and the decision is made to return it through the Gate. However, the orb suddenly shoots bolts across the room, pinning O'Neill to the wall through his shoulder. Organisms begin to infect both O'Neill and crucial SGC computer systems, and all attempts to destroy the orb worsen the situation and the Colonel's condition. As the organisms initiate the base self-destruct countdown, Carter suggests they try to communicate with the device.

Teal'c to O'Neill

"Undomesticated equines could not remove me."

"... That's a joke. You told a joke... don't make me laugh."

"You know those time capsules that we put together, so however many thousands of years from now, civilisations can see what we were all about?" asks co-writer Michael Greenburg. "Well, my big 'what if' with this episode was, 'what if another planet built a time capsule, but instead of a box, it was an orb that actually contained *everything* about that planet? All the information about the peoples, the technology — even its surviving beings — were somehow put in this orb. But it wasn't just an historical interest thing — the reason the whole world went into the orb was because the planet was unfit to live on any more. Diminishing returns had hit the planet, and they had to abandon their ways.' Kind of what would happen to Earth if we just ran it helter-skelter without any conservation or environmental awareness. So, their world was dead, and the team find the orb and bring it back — and it likes Earth and wants to stay! That was the seed of the idea and we just played off that. I wrote this story with Jarrad Paul, with whom I've written before on a couple of features. Then Brad Wright wrote the teleplay and did a phenomenal job. Rick also did a fantastic job, because he was impaled on a wall for most of the episode and it was tough! But the tough ones are always worth it in the end."

Supervisor John Gajdecki and co-ordinator Simon Lacey worked

on the visual effects for the episode, and colleague James Tichenor is full of praise for the results they achieved: "There's a shot where one of the legs of the device shoots through O'Neill's shoulder and pins him back to the wall. That was done with stunt man Dan Shea attached to an ascender rig that drove him into the wall, and we took a shot of him looking into the camera and then looking down again. We then mapped Rick's face from a green screen shoot onto Dan's body — so it's really a head replacement.

"From a practical point of view," Tichenor continues, "the luminous stuff you see when the organism takes over was really goo — technical term! — painted over the cast and props. The director of photography Peter Woest shot it using black light [ultra-violet to the rest of us] which made it glow in the dark." λ

Above: O'Neill and Teal'c restrain their sense of humour.

Family

Written by: Katharyn Powers	Guest cast: Teryl Rothery (Dr Fraiser), Tony Amendola
Directed by: William Gereghty	(Bra'tac), Peter Williams (Apophis), Brook Parker
	(Drey'auc), Neil Denis (Rya'c), Peter Bryant (Fro'tak),
	Jan Frandsen (Dj'nor), Laara Sadiq (Female Technician)

SG-1 travel to Teal'c's home world of Chulak when they learn that his son has been kidnapped by Apophis, who was presumed dead. However, Teal'c's homecoming and family reunion is not quite as he expected. His wife Drey'auc has re-married and when they find his son, Rya'c, he has been brainwashed by the System Lord and brands his own father a traitor. Teal'c finds danger and betrayal at every turn as family and old friends turn against him.

Helped by Bra'tac, the Jaffa's former mentor, the team struggle to de-programme the boy, outwit Apophis and restore familial relations.

Fro'tak to O'Neill

"I am Fro'tak of the High Cliffs."

"Jack — of the Windy City."

Christopher Judge remembers this episode specifically because it gave him another chance to work with Tony Amendola as Bra'tac, Teal'c's Jaffa mentor. "Tony is just 'The Man'," says Judge. "He has a real presence. It's a pleasure to share a scene with him." Judge is also pleased with the way the writers approached the tensions between Teal'c and his family: "I loved the way you got to see Teal'c display some strong emotion there. You really saw him being jealous and saw what lengths he would go to, to save his family and keep them together." Describing the scene in which Teal'c tried to attack his former best

The Original Apophis

Nastier than your average System Lord, Apophis is the quintessential personification of Goa'uld evil, with a particular spite for the SG-1 team, who seem to thwart his every attempt at world domination. He's had the same sort of bad luck throughout the ages, as Apophis in Greek mythology, and Apep in ancient Egypt. The Egyptians believed that the snake god rampaged through the night trying to stop Ra's sun from rising each day but, apart from the odd solar eclipse, he never quite managed to block out the light. The serpent was eventually killed by his arch enemy, who chopped his body into little pieces and sent his remains up in flames.

friend for running off with his wife, Judge laughs, "We had a little 'discussion' and O'Neill had to step in and calm the situation but hell, the guy deserved it." Asked if he really got into the part, and stalked around being rotten to the poor actor who had to cross him, Judge grins, "Naw! There were no such shenanigans on that one. It was a big episode for me. I'm only a disruptive force when it's someone else's episode!

"In the beginning Teal'c was totally focussed on freeing his people," Judge notes. "By the time 'Family' comes around, it's more a case of putting his wife and son before anything else. Teal'c is very proud of the boy and refuses to believe that he could fall under Apophis's influence. Teal'c's persistence finally pays off when Rya'c fights the brain-washing."

As irrepressible as ever, Mr Judge winks, "When you see Teal'c turn and smile as he takes his family back through the gate, it's because he knows he's going off for some 'marital relations' — if you know what I'm saying…" ⋏

Above: Jaffa warriors on Chulak.

Secrets

Written by: Terry Curtis Fox
Directed by: Duane Clark

Guest cast: Peter Williams (Apophis), Carmen Argenziano (General Jacob Carter), Erick Avali (Kasuf), Vaitiare Bandera (Sha're), Douglas H. Arthurs (Heru-ur), Chris Owens (Armin Selig), Michael Tiernan (Ryn'tak)

The integrity of the Stargate project is at risk when a reporter tells O'Neill that he knows what goes on inside the mountain complex, and intends to announce this to the world at large. Meanwhile, Daniel travels back to Abydos with Teal'c to explain that he has failed to find Sha're, but is amazed to find her alive, well and living at home. His joy is short-lived when he learns that she is about to give birth to Apophis' child. Back on Earth, Sam struggles with the devastating news that her father, who knows nothing of his daughter's secret career and is trying to get her a place in the space programme, is suffering from cancer. Whilst O'Neill battles to maintain the secrecy of the Stargate project, and Sam tries to withhold the fact that she is more than an astrophysicist from her father, Daniel and Teal'c conspire to use Apophis's rivalry with another System Lord, Heru-ur, to help them escape.

O'Neill

"It's O'Neill with two 'l's. There is another Colonel O'Neil who spells his name with one 'l'. He has no sense of humour."

Many friendships deepened and new bonds were formed between the regulars and guest cast during the filming of this episode. "It was wonderful to meet Carmen Argenziano," beams Amanda Tapping. "We met at six in the morning, and by seven he was telling me his character had cancer. It was a heavily emotional scene and we had to connect, but it ended up much deeper than that. I ended up loving him. Right before the scene, I reached over and squeezed his hand and said, 'Right! Here we go.' And it went from there. Our relationship as characters grew into

Ammonet

Sha're's Goa'uld name has echoes in Earth history. According to Egyptian mythology, Ammaunet was one of eight primal beings of the Ogdoad. A creator deity paired with Amun — the serpent one — she was spoken of as being omnipresent but concealed, giving rise to her title 'The Hidden One'.

a genuine love between a father and daughter, much the same as it's done on a personal level. We spend time together whenever we can. I'm proud to say he and his family have welcomed me as their own and he's become part of my family."

Above: A Horus Guard searches for Apophis's child.

"I liked the way the story built on the relationship between Teal'c and Daniel," says Chris Judge, "showing the depth of a friendship where Teal'c would go to great lengths, including putting some of his own feelings on hold, to support his friend. There is also an intensity between Daniel and his wife Sha're, which was really beautiful. The thing that touched me most was the way it showed Daniel, an outcast somewhat like Teal'c, finding his true love only to lose her through no fault of his own. His determination to stay true to her and to fight to get her back is a powerful lesson. I really admire Shanks for his performance in that one." λ

Bane

Written by: Robert C. Cooper	Guest cast: Teryl Rothery (Dr Fraiser), Tom McBeath
Directed by: David Warry-Smith	(Colonel Maybourne), Colleen Rennison (Ally)

On a mission to BP63Q1, the team are attacked by a swarm of giant insects, one of which stings Teal'c before they can make it back through the Gate. On his return to Earth, the Jaffa undergoes a physical mutation brought on by the insect venom. The military brass see Teal'c's condition as a means of developing a powerful biological weapon and take him from the SGC for experimentation. Teal'c escapes from the transport carrying him to another base and goes on the run. Sick and in hiding from the NID, time is running out for the Jaffa and the rest of the world. Whilst the rest of SG-1 risk a return visit to the insect world to find a cure, it's left to a plucky young homeless girl who has befriended Teal'c to save the day.

O'Neill

"Those are bugs, sir. Big, ugly bugs."

"David Warry-Smith used one of the old Expo buildings as the futuristic structure on the insects' planet, and we added some matte paintings," explains John Smith. "Then we used the Versatile Shipyards building, which is one of the biggest shipyards in Canada. Chris's character holed up in there." But Smith mainly remembers one thing about 'Bane': the bug. "It was a huge problem actually," he confides, "because we couldn't get the thing to stick on his shoulder like it was supposed to, and it kept falling down. Then it had a bit of a problem flapping its wings. Every time it tried to do that things went a bit awry…" Chuckling, he goes on, "We CG'd it flying around the Gateroom with Rick blowing the hell out of everything. That was a lot of fun! It was one of the first CG animals we used. We made the model first, then matched it with CG. It turned out very well."

"We loved doing Christopher's make-up, and creating the cocoon was wonderful," recalls make-up supervisor Jan Newman. "We could have spent a lot of money trying to get that right, but Wray Douglas, special effects supervisor, came up with the idea of webbing and it was fabulous."

Not that actor Christopher Judge shares her enthusiasm. "That make-up was *not* a whole lot of fun," he recalls. "I hated having to sit still for hours having all those little bumps and boils put on. It took almost two hours each day to get it right. Jan Newman just wanted to

torture me! And the director," Judge moans, "he kept me lying around on that hard, cold floor. I really had to suffer for my art."

Judge wasn't the only one who found filming the episode somewhat uncomfortable. "There's a scene right at the end where my character soaks Daniel Jackson with a water gun," Judge remembers. "I couldn't resist doing it, and Michael Shanks had no idea what was coming. I pumped the thing up to the highest pressure and just let him have it. He was drenched, and it hurt too. The look on his face was really priceless! We used that first take in the final edit because it was just so perfect." ⅄

Above: A big, ugly bug from planet BP63Q1.

The Tok'ra [Part I]

Written by: Jonathan Glassner Directed by: Brad Turner	Guest cast: J. R. Bourne (Martouf), Carmen Argenziano (Jacob Carter), Sarah Douglas (Garshaw of Belote), Winston Rekert (Cordesh), Joy Coghill (Selmak), Steve Makaj (Colonel Makepeace), Laara Sadiq (Technician Davis)

Sam Carter experiences a vivid dream where she remembers events from the life of Jolinar, the Tok'ra who inhabited her body before being killed by a Goa'uld assassin. Despite the fact that her father is dying, Carter feels an irresistible urge to act on these dreams. So SG-1 head for the planet P34353J, trying to find the mysterious Tok'ra and forge an alliance. The first meeting, with a heavily armed Tok'ra patrol, does not run smoothly, with a high degree of mistrust on both sides. Relations remain tense, though the Tok'ra do reveal more about their practices and beliefs, like the fact that they do not use the Sarcophagus to prolong their lives. However, the potentially volatile situation is exacerbated when the Tok'ra invite one of the SG team to volunteer as a host to an important member of their tribe. Appalled at the very suggestion, the team decline the request. Assuming that the peoples of Earth have little of value to offer, the Tok'ra refuse an alliance and instead imprison SG-1, on the grounds that they would pose a security threat if allowed to return home. In the spirit of reconciliation, Carter and Martouf, who was Jolinar's partner for almost a hundred years, agree to spend time together, in an effort to find some common ground between the Earth dwellers and the Tok'ra.

O'Neill to Martouf

"OK, son. But you'd better have her back by 11'o'clock."

Asked to explain the ideas behind the creation of the Tok'ra, Jonathan Glassner begins, "They were an important invention that we really needed. We felt that the Goa'uld were becoming very one-dimensional. They were just bad, bad, bad. I kept thinking that there had to be rebels other than the odd Jaffa that didn't agree with what the Goa'uld were doing. But that raised all kinds of interesting questions, because they were still stealing people in order to live, so how good could they be? That's what started off the idea of willing hosts. We developed the three episode arc with Sam Carter's dad dying of cancer, which made him the perfect choice of somebody to be Tok'ra-ed."

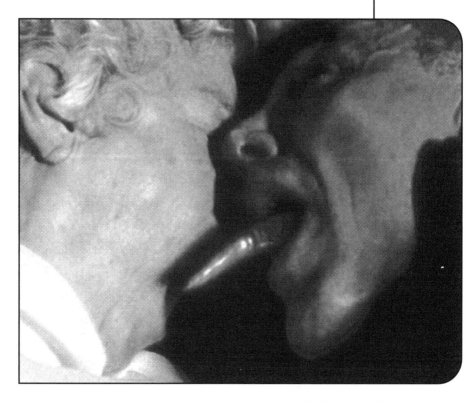

A mutual admiration society built up between Amanda Tapping and J. R. Bourne whilst filming 'The Tok'ra'. "It was incredible," recalls Bourne. "From the moment we met, it was as if I'd known this woman all my life. There's a scene where we take a walk and then sit down to talk about Jolinar, and it's the first time I've ever been in an 'acting' situation where I wasn't acting. It just seemed so natural walking along and chatting to her, that we were both surprised when the director yelled 'cut'." Tapping has similar memories of the episode: "The best thing was meeting J. R. Bourne — Martouf. We had virtually no time to learn this seven-page scene together, but he was so lovely it just seemed to flow. When we did the whole walking sequence through the desert I remember it being a huge wide shot, so you couldn't exactly see our mouths, but we were having a really great conversation. I can't recall what we were talking about now, but there was just this instant connection. It was the same as when I met Carmen on 'Secrets' and Tamsin Kelsey in 'Thor's Hammer'. We met at six am, and were telling each other our deepest, darkest secrets by lunchtime!" λ

Above: Mouth to mouth regeneration.

The Tok'ra (Part II)

Written by: Jonathan Glassner
Directed by: Brad Turner

Guest cast: J. R. Bourne (Martouf), Carmen Argenziano (Jacob Carter), Sarah Douglas (Garshaw of Belote), Winston Rekert (Cordesh), Joy Coghill (Selmak), Steve Makaj (Colonel Makepeace), Laara Sadiq (Technician Davis)

As negotiations between the two races continue to crumble, Carter comes up with a possible solution to help Earth and the Tok'ra. Her father is dying of cancer, but if he were to act as the new host, both lives could be saved. The Tok'ra agree to let her and O'Neill return through the Stargate. By the time she brings her sick father to the Tok'ra world the Goa'uld, having placed a spy within their midst, have located the rebels and launched a full scale attack. The union of Jacob Carter with Selmak gets underway as the battle rages around them, and a human/Tok'ra alliance is finally forged through a growing mutual respect and need for self-defence against the common enemy.

> **O'Neill**
>
> "Well General, if these were your everyday, run-of-the-mill, greasy-assed Goa'uld, they would've made us their hosts already."

Jonathan Glassner has nothing but praise for the efforts put in by the set designer and construction crew during 'The Tok'ra'. "That big round crystal set was quite an amazing invention," he notes. "They put it up, and about six or seven episodes later we needed it again. The problem was that, because of the way the set was made, they couldn't fold and store it. They'd trashed it, and had to reproduce it from scratch so we could use the crystal set again. However, the second time, they constructed it so that the set could be used over and over again. Which was a damn good thing, as we writers knew we'd be going back to the Tok'ra." Teased that there must have been a lot of frustrated swearing going on at the time in the construction department, Glassner jokes, "Naw! It was easier for them to build the second time, when they knew what they were doing!"

As writer, Glassner is personally proud of the scene when Jacob Carter receives the Goa'uld for the first time, saying, "I thought it was a very touching scene between him and the old lady." Fans and critics alike commented that it was an extremely brave move to show two people who weren't young, blonde slips of things kissing on screen. "Well,

she had to be a dying, *old* lady," laughs Glassner, "and you don't see too many cute, young versions of those." Glassner also reveals that the later return of the Jacob character was down to the executive producers falling in love with the actor involved. "We liked Carmen Argenziano so much we had to change our plans," he says. "We didn't intend bringing Jacob back after this episode, but having worked with Carmen we thought he was excellent, and just had to write more for him."

The writers tried to do the same for British actress Sarah Douglas, but sadly other commitments prevented her return in the second season. "Sarah was a fantastic baddie in *V* and *Superman II*, and we wanted to play it so that it could look as though she were a bad guy — playing on the mistrust thing. She's very strong, yet very feminine. I love the look on Jack O'Neill's face when she kisses him near the end of the episode." λ

Above: Garshaw of Belote stands her ground.

Spirits

Written by: Tor Alexander Valenza
Directed by: Martin Wood

Guest cast: Rodney A. Grant (Tonane), Roger Cross (Captain Conner), Alex Zahara (Xe'ls), Christina Cox (T'akaya), Kevin McNulty (Dr Warner), Laara Sadiq (Technician Davis)

A s SG-1 prepare to go through the Stargate in search of SG-11, who have not returned from a mission, a Trinium-tipped arrow flies out of the open Gate, injuring O'Neill. Carter is placed in charge and the remaining three travel to a planet inhabited by Salish Indians. It is a world full of mystery and legend, and SG-1 discover that the missing unit have apparently been abducted by the animal Spirits who are the guardians of the Salish. When SG-11 suddenly reappear, both teams return home, bringing an Indian called Tonane with them in an attempt to strike a mining deal for Trinium. However, the members of SG-11 are not all they seem, and when lies lead to mistrust, the full fury of the Spirits is unleashed.

> ### O'Neill
> "Brace yourselves, SG-11 is bopping around waving their arms together making our people disappear."

"In all honesty, 'Spirits' was one of those episodes that had some great ideas, and some really interesting moral arguments, and which read far better on paper than it ended up playing out. Which is probably why you don't hear an awful lot about it," observes Michael Shanks. "It was part of our experimental phase that we were going through as we investigated how we as SG-1, and also the audience, would react to off-shoots of different cultures. And I don't think that story was a particularly sensitive approach to the subject matter in hand." Without wishing to dismiss the episode entirely, Shanks candidly remarks, "I just don't think we pulled it off terribly well. We had other things on our mind, because it came around the time when Richard Dean Anderson's child was due to be born, so a lot of re-writes were being done at the last minute to remove him from the story. The part where we go to the planet without O'Neill was done for a specific reason. Rick's partner Apryl was due to go into the hospital, and we panicked and changed lines to allow him to go with her. So as a result, the usual team dynamic just wasn't there. It wasn't the worst episode in the world, but I think we'd all like to draw a veil over that one."

The production had to substitute a few animals as well as humans

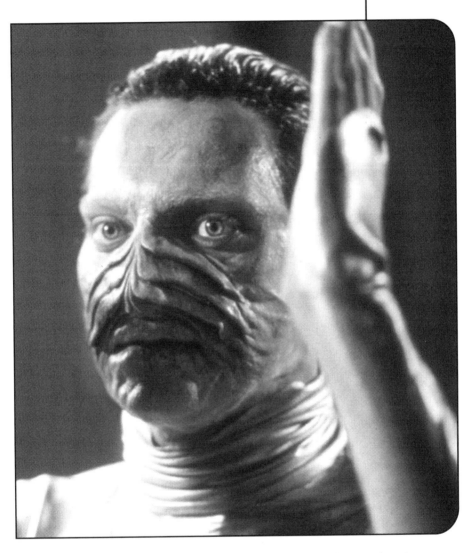

during the shooting of 'Spirits'. According to Jonathan Glassner, "We were going to use a bear instead of a wolf, but in British Columbia it's illegal to work with trained animals that are originally from the wild. As we couldn't get a real bear or wolf, we actually went with a mixed breed of half wolf and half German Shepherd." Tongue firmly in cheek he suggests, "Basically, they had sex in the wild, where probably a wolf attacked a domestic dog, and this was the off-spring. So that was legal and we were able to use that!" ⅄

Above: A spirit reveals its true appearance.

Touchstone

Written by: Sam Egan	Guest cast: Tom McBeath (Colonel Maybourne),
Directed by: Brad Turner	Matthew Walker (Roham), Jerry Wasserman (Whitlow),
	Tiffany Knight (La Moor), Eric Breker (Major Reynolds)

A device capable of controlling an entire world's climate is stolen from a paradise-like planet by a team posing as SG-1. As the weather on Madrona starts to deteriorate, it is up to the real SG-1 to locate the missing Touchstone and identify the thieves. Their investigations result in the disturbing news that Earth's second Stargate has been reactivated, and is being used by a 'black ops' group whose motives are highly suspect. SG-1 enter a race against time to find out just how high this deception goes in the chain of US Military command, while trying to recover the Touchstone before the inhabitants of Madrona perish.

O'Neill

"We came in peace. We expect to go in one piece."

It was a very special week for Michael Shanks, and the actor can only think of one event when asked to reminisce. "The thing that stands out the most from that episode for me personally, is that 'Touchstone' is the one we were filming when my child was born," he says. "It was 10 August 1998. To me the episode was a blur, because I was practising breathing technique, then going through all that new father angst!" Smiling at the memory he teases, "The blowing snow scene was one thing I do remember. That was interesting, but I have to admit that, though I didn't exactly ignore what was going on around me at work, I

Stormy Weather

The King in 'Touchstone' has a special supernatural device that enables him to control his world's weather system. Throughout the history of our own planet, various monarchs and family heads have done their best to get the tides to literally turn in their favour. The most famous is probably King Canute, a chap so obsessed with his own self-importance that he thought he could make the mighty ocean do his bidding, and turn away from the shore. Inevitably, he ended up by getting more than his feet wet. Shakespeare's King Lear had a go too — ranting and raving at the winds and waves, and though not royalty in the fullest sense, Prospero was monarch of all he surveyed, and could conjure up a fair old tempest.

was pretty distracted. My mind was somewhere else at that point…"

The references in the episode to Area 51, the real-life, ultra-top-secret Air Force base in the Nevada desert, caused some problems with the powers-that-be, who proved rather sensitive. "Originally, in the script, we had O'Neill saying something like, 'Is this where we keep the little green men?'" Jonathan Glassner reveals. "But the Air Force has full approval of all our scripts, and they called and said, 'There are no aliens in Area 51. You can't keep that line in.' I explained that it was a joke, but they just repeated, 'There are no aliens in Area 51.' So I then asked if I could use their response in the script! We actually ended up going with O'Neill saying, 'Is this where they keep the aliens?' and the officer replies, 'There are no aliens in Area 51.' Then O'Neill looks at Teal'c and says, 'Present company excluded.'" Λ

Above: The King of Madrona holds the Touchstone.

A Matter of Time

Story by: Misha Rashovich
Teleplay by: Brad Wright
Directed by: Jimmy Kaufman

Guest cast: Marshal Teague (Colonel Cromwell), Teryl Rothery (Dr Fraiser), Tobias Mehler (Lieutenant Graham Simmons), Dan Shea (Sergeant Siler)

Whilst on a reconnaissance trip to P3X451, SG-10 encounters a spatial irregularity — a black hole which quickly engulfs the planet. An attempt to rescue them fails, but by activating the Stargate on Earth the door is literally left open for the black hole's gravitational pull to exert its deadly influence on the Stargate Command Centre. As time comes to a near standstill, one member of SG-1 in particular must put aside past differences in order to help Sam Carter deflect the looming catastrophe.

Cromwell

"Is that proper military terminology? What is 'funky'?"

Occasionally people will say that their world has been turned upside down, but it was more a case of the world being turned on its side in 'A Matter of Time'. "Trying to build all the sets sideways gave the production team something to think about all right!" laughs John Smith. "We literally had to build a replica of the Gateroom turned on its side, so that we could have the two guys dangling from a rope. The ropes were particularly problematic too. In theory they were meant to be hanging loose but they weren't, we had them stretched out as tight as they could be and then we turned the camera sideways so that it looked right side up."

It certainly wasn't a picnic for the guys in question, who had to hang on for the best part of a day. "When we did 'A Matter of Time', that really is Ricky [Dean Anderson] and me up there on the ropes," recalls guest actor Marshall Teague. "We were about twenty or thirty feet off the ground, and there was no stunt man on that. Rick did all his own work — the inversion, the fall, the whole works." Explaining that he had the benefit of mountain climbing training in his childhood days, Teague grins, "When I was much younger, I went on a course run by the National Leadership School, where you traipse off into the Grant Teton Mountains in the US for a month. You live off granola, what you pick up off the ground and what you can steal — sorry, borrow — from anybody else, and they teach you mountain climbing. So, I've been climbing for a lot of my life. As for ol' MacGyver — well, that guy can do anything!" On a serious note, Teague praises the stamina and ability of his fellow actor: "Rick is very agile and very athletic, although neither of us

was particularly thrilled about being in a harness all day. It's pretty hard on the back."

Above: O'Neill and Cromwell *prepare to save the day.*

Although *Stargate SG-1* is noted for often having a less than serious approach to science fiction, Brad Wright feels that "every now and then we do use a straight-ahead science fiction 'high concept'. I don't think we could get away with shoot-em-up episodes every week. 'A Matter of Time' was one of those stories where we used a sci-fi staple — in this case a black hole, and all the phenomena associated with that — and built the episode around it." λ

The Fifth Race

Written by: Robert C. Cooper	Guest cast: Teryl Rothery (Dr Fraiser), Tobias
Directed by: David Warry-Smith	Mehler (Lieutenant Graham Simmons), Dan Shea
	(Sergeant Siler)

When Jack O'Neill's inquisitive nature gets the better of him and he peers into an alien viewing device, he gets far more than he bargained for. His brain is instantly filled with a vast amount of data that gives him the ability to decipher base eight maths, design complicated machinery and speak in a foreign tongue. Unfortunately, these admirable skills come at a price, as human brains aren't yet far enough advanced to cope with such a download of software. With his brain rapidly failing, it becomes clear that O'Neill must leave his companions and travel through the Stargate alone in an effort to save himself. Having built a device which provides a huge surge of power to the Stargate, O'Neill sets the co-ordinates to an address which is off the starcharts. The Colonel's solo trip leads to an encounter which gives hope to more than one race in the galaxy…

> **O'Neill**
>
> "I've lost the falatus to speak properly."

Visual effects supervisor James Tichenor's favourite shot in 'The Fifth Race' is "the big effect right at the beginning, when O'Neill gets his head stuck in the little contraption. That was an effect where we morphed between the 'open' position, with O'Neill getting stuck, and the 'closed' position, where the whole thing wrapped around his head.

The Asgard

These small grey aliens from the planet Othala in the galaxy of Ida were once part of the Alliance, a conglomerate of four great races comprising the Asgard, the Nox, the Furlings and the Ancients (the builders of the Stargates). Although the Alliance is now defunct, the Asgard still strenuously oppose Goa'uld plans to dominate the universe. They are also determined upholders of the Protected Planets Treaty, which prevents the Goa'uld from attacking the inhabitants of certain worlds. Earth is on the verge of becoming such a planet. Having observed humans for some time, the Asgard feel that we have taken our first steps towards universal advancement, and could well become the Fifth Race.

Above: O'Neill, about to become the fount of all knowledge.

It was a classic 2D CG morph, where it looked like the device came out and wrapped around him. If you look closely enough," Tichenor continues, revealing a few trade secrets, "you can actually see the point where we had to morph Rick's head as well, because when you have two different elements like that, sometimes it's difficult to make it look like the actor is actually interacting with the CG element in the shot. When the device was in its 'open' position, and hadn't wrapped round Rick's head all the way, he would have had to stay utterly stock still during filming to allow us to achieve the effect properly — it was easier to make his head CG as well! Then, when it was in the 'closed' position, we can't see Rick at all because the thing is covering his face. We had to spend a lot of time considering how we were going to cover both sides, and what was the most cost efficient way of doing it. It seems like a pretty simple shot, but it took a lot of effort to get it looking that interesting. It almost has the feeling of a hand coming out of the wall. It's cool!" ⅄

Serpent's Song

Written by: Katharyn Powers	Guest cast: Teryl Rothery (Dr Fraiser), Peter Williams
Directed by: Peter DeLuise	(Apophis), J. R. Bourne (Martouf), Tobias Mehler
	(Lieutenant Graham Simmons), Peter Lacroix (Ashrak)

ntrigued by a mysterious signal asking for parlance, SG-1 travel to a desert world, where they witness a damaged spaceship plunge to the ground in a ball of flame. Amongst the wreckage they discover a battered and bleeding Apophis, who begs for sanctuary. Back on Earth it becomes apparent that their adversary is dying but, in return for a new host, the Snake tempts them with the offer of all the knowledge he has at his disposal. O'Neill refuses to allow any such transfer, whereupon the duplicitous Apophis reveals that he is being hunted down by his arch enemy Sokar, who will stop at nothing to retrieve his prey. Martouf of the Tok'ra advises his friends to return one evil System Lord to the other, or risk being destroyed.

> **Daniel to Apophis**
>
> "I know where your son is."

"When I was invited to direct the episode," says Peter DeLuise, "first off I was reminded of a movie called *Brian's Song*, which was an ode to a football player who is slowly dying. In 'Serpent's Song' I was moved by the title, because I realised we were going to help Apophis die. He'd subjected everyone to a season and a half of arch enemy-type things, he was not loved, and each member of SG-1 was given an opportunity to have a scene with him to say goodbye. The most interesting thing for me was that it was my first episode, and I had to watch pretty much every single one before that to get a real feel for the show, and know exactly how everything was interplaying.

"Peter Williams had to age over the course of the show, and we used these great leg braces, an idea which I 'borrowed' from the movie *Crash*," DeLuise continues. "I thought I should bind him tight, like Hannibal Lecter, to denote him as a dangerous enemy, but in the script I had fourteen pages of him in the hospital room and realised, 'Well, this could potentially be very boring', so I wanted to do something interesting with it. Peter Williams, God bless him, had the cataract lenses put over his eyes, he was in old age make-up, he was in a strait-jacket and his legs were bound. He was completely tied down, couldn't move at all. He did a wonderful job of staying Zen-like and never lost his cool. Every

time I talked to him I would touch his arm, because I was conscious that I was talking to a blind person who was not used to being blind, which could have been very disconcerting for him."

Above: Apophis demands sanctuary.

Whilst that is all very laudable, Peter Williams reveals the director played at least one practical joke on him. "At the very end of the episode, after the last scene was shot, Peter had everyone shut down the cameras, turn out the lights and just walk off the set," Willams recalls. "I was still strapped to the gurney! I lay there calling out, 'Guys?' for several minutes before they came back and let me in on the joke. I still haven't figured out how to pay him back for that one..." λ

Holiday

Written by: Tor Alexander Valenza Directed by: David Warry-Smith	Guest cast: Michael Shanks (Machello), Teryl Rothery (Dr Fraiser)

The SG-1 team are exploring chambers belonging to Machello, an apparently harmless senior citizen who is the creator and guardian of a wealth of technology designed to defeat the dreaded Goa'uld. Appealing to Daniel's inquisitive nature, the alien manages to trick the young archaeologist into using a 'body swapping' machine. On their return to Earth, Machello uses Daniel's body to embark on a voyage of discovery, enjoying many physical and sensory pleasures sacrificed during his interminable battle with the Goa'uld. In an attempt to assist their friend, now confined to a hospital bed, trapped in Machello's dying alien body, Teal'c and O'Neill bring the machine to Stargate Command. But they accidentally trigger the device, and switch bodies themselves. Machello is finally tracked down, and brought back to Cheyenne mountain, where he reveals that his machine's process is irreversible...

> ### Daniel
> "Nice to know you don't just like me for my looks."

Michael Shanks has a quiet chuckle as he recounts his memories as Daniel Jackson's *alter-alter ego*. "There are lots of little things about 'Holiday' that make me smile," he recalls. "For a start it was the best episode on paper that I had read for the show. It was very complete from an actor's perspective. Playing both those roles looked as though it was going to be a tough task, but I was really looking forward to doing it.

"It *was* daunting, though," he continues. "I was playing two separate characters (and I do consider Daniel to be a character — he is *not* me), then having them switch bodies and allowing their two very different personalities to shine through. Not to mention having my own personality that I began with being converted from who *I* am in the first place."

Confused? He was! Laughing outright Shanks adds, "You then have to converse with yourself and have them talking to themselves as each other! I looked at the script and thought, 'This is pretty much the hardest thing I've ever had to do...'" Modest about his performance, Shanks

thinks "with hindsight, I would have done things a lot differently and done a much better job. But it was one of those opportunities that you rarely get on episodic television and I went for it."

Above: Three men in a body.

The actor is full of praise for the make-up team however: "We had such a good prosthetic guy he deserved an award. Even the head of MGM at the time didn't realise it was me. We had to tell him later at a dinner. John Symes was complimenting Rick on playing Chris's character and Michael Greenburg said, 'Yeah! And how about Michael playing the old man?'" Apparently Symes kept staring at Shanks, waiting for the punch-line: "He'd watched the episode and didn't know it was me under all that make-up!"

Shanks remembers that one of his favourite scenes came at the end of the show, "when we all got to jump into each other's bodies and I got to play Jack O'Neill for a few shining moments." Asked if he had to study long and hard to get into the part, Shanks reveals with a laugh, "Oh, I think by that point we knew each other well enough to be able to pretty much pull off decent impersonations of one another at any given moment!" ⋏

One False Step

Written by: Michael Kaplan and John Sanborn Directed by: William Corcoran	Guest cast: Teryl Rothery (Dr Fraiser), Colin Heath (Technician)

When a UAV crashes during a routine reconnaissance flight on an alien world, it sets off a chain of events that could mean the destruction of a simple and friendly race of beings. When SG-1 visit the planet to recover the remote control plane, they are horrified as members of the alien race start to collapse and fall into a coma-like state at an alarming rate. Before long, O'Neill and Jackson appear to be suffering adverse effects too, but they recover completely once they return to Earth. Acting on a hunch, Carter sets about finding a cure before the illness spreads, and Earth's off-world activities become responsible for the destruction of an entire alien civilisation.

Jackson to Teal'c

"Can you keep an eye on this plant thing for us?"

"I will keep both eyes on it, Daniel Jackson."

"That was the episode with the stranger-than-usual costumes and the little huts," recalls producer John Smith. "We shot 'One False Step' out in a place called Stokestead, and we specifically went to that area because it's notoriously drier than the rest of Vancouver. It had to be that way to get an authentic feel to the landscape, especially for the surveillance images where the little plane is flying around photographing the big plants that come out of the ground."

Diplomatic as they come, Smith smiles, "It was really interesting when we cast that one. Without wishing to offend anyone, we really needed 'different'-looking people, and as far as the costumes were concerned we went with a sort of mime look, in that the performers looked like basic mime artistes, with the skin suit and white make-up. It turned out pretty good with the whole look of the set, the location, the costumes and the powdered make-up, but the weather was a constant concern. We spent the whole time worried that there would be a torrential downpour. This region is subject to that kind of occurrence without any warning so we thought, 'What the hell are we going to do with these guys if it pours? If they get rain drops on them we're done for!' We got lucky," laughs Smith. "The gods smiled on us and it stayed dry."

"All the actors and background cast were shaved bald and fitted

Above: The natives investigate an odd looking creature.

into a flesh-tone body-suit designed by Christina McQuarrie," make-up supervisor Jan Newman recalls. "The suits had various body markings that were continued onto the hands, feet and faces. Six make-up artists worked on the characters over the six days, each taking about one hour per character. They were all great people to work with!"

Teryl Rothery has fond memories of 'One False Step' because it gave her the chance to jump through the Stargate. "They had made reference to my going off-world in a previous episode, but this was the first time anyone saw me go through. I loved it. The scene that always makes me smile is where Janet steps through the Gate, all five foot two of her, bulked up in a full hazard suit, dwarfed by two burly medical guys. Her first words are, 'Now this is what I call a house call.' It cracks me up." ⋏

Show and Tell

Written by: Jonathan Glassner Directed by: Peter DeLuise	Guest cast: Teryl Rothery (Dr Fraiser), Carmen Argenziano (Jacob Carter), Jeff Gulka (Charlie)

The Stargate self-activates, and despite all attempts to seal the iris, a solitary figure appears in SGC — a young boy who announces that he has come to warn the people of Earth of their impending doom. The child belongs to a race called the Reetou, and he reveals that his mother has been at SGC for some time, but has remained invisible to human eyes. 'Charlie' has been created in human form to serve as an intermediary between the two races, but a faction of invisible rebel Reetou are also here, intent on destroying all life forms who are potential hosts for the Goa'uld. General Hammond decides it's time to call on his allies the Tok'ra for assistance.

Teal'c

"If there is a Reetou in this room, it came through the Stargate and it is capable of controlling the iris."

Peter DeLuise says he's used to working with kids and animals, or kids and insects as it was in this case. "We used the little boy who plays Gibson Praise in *The X-Files*. He's got a great look. He was bald and we painted some veins on his skin to make him look more fragile, but he's a lot older than he looks. He was about thirteen." Admitting that he's a bit of big kid himself, DeLuise laughs, "One of the ways I tried to endear myself to Jeff [Gulka] was by buying him a video game, so that he would know I was 'cool'. But he was *way* beyond that. He was into video games quite a lot, but he was just getting into girls at that point…"

Boys and girls aside, the director says that he thoroughly enjoyed making an appearance in the episode: "I played the machine gun guard in that one. I'm in quite a few episodes but I've started putting myself in in sneakier ways. You have to look out for various parts of my anatomy now." Mr DeLuise doesn't specify which.

"We gave Peter a shot at directing on *Stargate SG-1* and haven't looked back," comments Jonathan Glassner. "He started off directing one show and is now creative consultant. He is so full of energy and loves the show so much that it's great." Brad Wright agrees with Glassner's assessment of the effervescent Mr DeLuise: "He would come in every five minutes saying, 'I got this great idea!' or 'How about we do this?' Making him creative consultant seemed as good a way as any to get him out of my office and into his own."

Stargate SG-1's other Peter, Peter Williams, smiles, "Peter DeLuise is generous with his good fortune. He has this little 'thing' where he will come up and ask you a question about any episode, and if you answer correctly he'll throw you a two-dollar piece. Being struggling actors, of course, we are grateful for all donations. None of the cast ever give it back!" Λ

Above: O'Neill offers paternal protection.

1969

Written by: Brad Wright	Guest cast: Alex Zahara (Michael), Aaron Pearl
Directed by: Charles Correll	(Lieutenant George Hammond), Amber Rothwell
	(Jenny), Pamela Perry (Cassandra), Glynis Davies
	(Catherine), Fred Henderson (Major Thornbird)

General Hammond hands Carter a letter as the team heads off on their latest mission. As they pass through the Gate, a solar flare reconfigures their trajectory and they end up back on Earth but in the year 1969. Arrested as spies and later aided by a young George Hammond, who is instructed to help them in the letter written by his older self, the team must locate the Stargate before the next solar flare, or they may be stuck in the past forever. As they race cross-country to find the Gate, they are given a ride by a young couple *en route* to Woodstock.

O'Neill and Jackson

"We came to Earth to hide among your people a long, long time ago..."

"... from a galaxy far, far away."

Just the mention of '1969', the episode and the year, brings a smile to Michael Greenburg's face: "I was eighteen in 1969. That episode's amongst my top three or four in the whole series. Brad wrote it. He was only eight in 1969, but he has a great sensibility for the time. It was fun being back in that era, with the Magic Bus and the funky wardrobe and the vibe. Rick and the whole cast really bought into it — we just had a blast filming that story." As well as waxing lyrical about the time, Greenburg is very complimentary about the way Jim Menard, the director of photography, filmed the episode: "He did a brilliant job. My favourite is the shot in the armoury hall when the crate falls away revealing the Stargate. That was beautifully lit. In film-making terms it really was spectacular."

"It was out-and-out fun time!" recalls Brad Wright. "After the success of 'Tin Man' in season one, we decided to try for at least one episode every season that's just plain fun. What I love about '1969' is that it doesn't take itself too seriously. That's something we've consciously tried to avoid with *Stargate SG-1*. One of the things that makes us different from a lot of the other shows on television is our ability to laugh at ourselves, and be a little bit off-beat every now and then. I think most of our audience appreciates that."

Production designer Richard Hudolin certainly did. More used to

Above: Sam and Daniel – Far Out and Solid.

dealing with the weird and wonderful in other worlds, he was glad of the opportunity to keep his sandals on the ground. "A lot of the people who work on the show are of that era," he points out, "so we all really got into the swing of things."

If the groovy music wafting SG-1 along the highway sounds partic-ularly cool, it's because it was composed by Bruce Turgon, of the rock band Foreigner. A friend of Michael Greenburg and great fan of the show, Turgon wrote and performed the accompaniment for the 'on the road' part of the episode. ⅄

Out of Mind

Story by: Jonathan Glassner and Brad Wright **Teleplay by:** Jonathan Glassner **Directed by:** Martin Wood	Guest cast: Teryl Rothery (Dr Fraiser), Suanne Braun (Hathor), Tom Butler (Major General Trofsky), Samantha Ferris (Dr Raully)

O'Neill awakens from a cryogenic state to be told he has been frozen for almost eighty years and that the rest of his team is dead. As he tries to come to terms with what has happened, the Colonel begins to suspect that all may not be as it seems, and that the unfamiliar people around him may not be SGC staff as they claim. His fears are confirmed when he overhears the doctors talking in Goa'uld, and discovers that he and the rest of his team are in fact being held in a Goa'uld interrogation stronghold. In command is one of their fiercest enemies — Hathor — who is determined one of the team should be host to her next First Prime.

O'Neill

"What, the grey doesn't bother you?"

"What's funny about 'Out of Mind' is that none of us on the show particularly liked the character of Hathor," begins Jonathan Glassner. "In fact, Richard Dean Anderson *really* didn't like her — and it shows." Emphasising that Anderson *did* like and had great respect for Suanne Braun, the actress who portrayed the goddess, Glassner goes on, "We came up with 'Out Of Mind', which was just such a great idea, but soon realised that the only Goa'uld we could use was Hathor. In the whole mythology we'd created with the Goa'uld, she was the only one we had at the time that we'd developed who had a chance of still being out there and alive. So I went up to Rick and said, 'Let me tell you this really cool story,' and he listened and replied, 'Oh that's really cool.' Then I went, 'There's only one catch. The Goa'uld is Hathor.' Rick gave me such a glare but I insisted, 'So what do you think? It's the only way.' He took another couple of seconds before groaning, 'Oh OK! Go ahead.'

"She was an on-going joke between us for the whole time," Glassner continues. "We'd be having discussions about where to take various ideas and I'd say, 'Come on! I've done some great shows with' and he'd just look and go — 'Hathor!'" Showing that torture is alive and thriving on the *Stargate* set, Glassner smirks, "There's a website on the Internet where fans rate their favourite episodes and well into

the second season, the highest-rated was always 'Hathor'. So natural-ly I kept rubbing this in Richard Dean Anderson's face and every so often would pop my head round his door and tease, 'Oh Rick, guess what's number one again this week?' It used to drive him crazy!

Above: Carter and O'Neill try to elude the Goa'uld.

"I don't know why 'Hathor' was such a well-liked story," Glassner concludes, "but I guess it was a firm favourite amongst the more fem-inist fans, because the women at SGC got to kick ass and save the day." Without wishing to detract from the opinion of the executive producer, it could be argued that the episode's popularity amongst female fans has something to do with the fact O'Neill and Daniel get to take their shirts off!

Reservations aside, Hathor proved to be a more than worthy adver-sary for the team, bringing about season's two's memorable cliffhanger, as she prepares to implant Jack with a Goa'uld larvae… ⋏

Colonel Jack O'Neill

"Next time I want to help someone, feel free to give a swift kick."

T alking with Richard Dean Anderson on set in Vancouver, it's hard to distinguish where the actor ends and Colonel Jack O'Neill begins, because they're men with a very similar take on life. Open, straightforward, charming and disarming, both men have a special job to do, don't deviate from their task and yet manage to inject a distinct sense of levity into the proceedings. "We try not to take ourselves too seriously," he smiles. "We do explore some contentious issues on the show, and often investigate the more serious of life's aspects, but we try to keep a lightness and a sense of humour about the whole approach."

Asked why he decided to take on the dual roles of executive producer and leading actor in the series, the ex-*MacGyver* star shrugs, "Because I hadn't. Done a science fiction show that is. I'd always said I'd try anything once, and when this opportunity presented itself it seemed the right time for a foray into the realms of science fiction."

Stargate SG-1's première episode sees O'Neill dragged out of voluntary retirement to head up a motley crew of experts, including an anthropologist, an astrophysicist and a chap from a galaxy far, far away. The first defence against a hoard of marauding predators, the newly-formed unit proceed to regularly throw themselves through a watery portal in order to seek out new worlds and civilisations, in the hope that someone, somewhere will share the technology and knowledge needed to defeat the Goa'uld.

"When I looked at the film I liked the character of O'Neil [played by Kurt Russell], but knew I'd have to do things differently," Anderson recalls of his approach to the role. So, as well as a slight difference in the spelling of his name (a fact touched on in the second season's 'Secrets', when Anderson's character quips, "There is another Colonel O'Neil, who spells his name with one 'l'") the characters couldn't be more dissimilar. There's still an initial animosity between the key players in the series, for example O'Neill makes it clear in 'Children of the Gods' that he has "a problem with scientists". He thinks the anthropologist in his team is a geek (Daniel Jackson notes this in his diary in 'Fire and Water'), and he gets 'weirded out' by Teal'c, as evidenced by an off-the-cuff remark made during 'Need'. However, the Colonel's leadership skills, such as they are — "I think this is supposed to be where I say some-

thing profound — nothing comes to mind. Let's go!" he says in 'Within the Serpent's Grasp' — and obvious concern for his 'kids', brings the team together.

A consummate action man, Richard Dean Anderson's road to *Stargate SG-1* has thrown a few energetic challenges in his path. Having set his heart on becoming a professional hockey player (a dream shared by colleague Michael Shanks), Anderson had to abandon that ambition when he broke both his arms. Undaunted, he embarked on an epic bike ride across North America. *En route* he fought forest fires in British Columbia, a role he claims as one of his most rewarding to date, and also worked as a whale trainer in California. He enjoyed some wild times as a DJ whilst at college in Ohio, and sparkled as a jester-singer-mime-juggler in a sixteenth century Renaissance-style cabaret in Los Angeles. All stuff that should come in pretty handy when it's time to entertain the true love of his life — his daughter Wylie.

For a man who seems to flit from experience to experience, Anderson exhibits extreme staying power when it comes to television shows. Cast as Dr Jeff Webber in *General Hospital*, he continued in the role of American daytime TV's medical heartthrob for five years. He then became the focus of international attention when his even longer run as *MacGyver* went into worldwide syndication. The part called for Anderson to play "an intellectual-type adventurer — a kind of Indiana Jones. Henry Winkler was the co-producer on the show. He told me I got the part as soon as I put my glasses on to read the script."

Although he admits that after the seven-year stint on *MacGyver* "everyone was getting a little tired and ready to move on to the next challenge", Anderson went on to make two highly successful *MacGyver* films with business partner Michael Greenburg. The two also executive produced the critically acclaimed series *Legend*. With tongue firmly in cheek Anderson warns, "Don't get me started on *Legend*. It was one of the best projects I've ever been involved in and damn it, I'm a little bitter that it didn't continue." The show was an entertaining piece of nonsense about a journalist with a fantastic *alter ego*. Given that the subject matter would endear it to media types all over the world, this particular journalist agrees *Legend*'s demise is a crying shame. Luckily, *Stargate SG-1* was just around the corner to take Anderson's mind off it.

As for Jack O'Neill's life journey to Stargate Command — that's a story best left to the man himself...

Memo from Colonel O'Neill
By Richard Dean Anderson

I'll just start where it gets interesting for me. The kid stuff, in retrospect, seems normal by any objective perspective: mom and dad divorced, sibling rivalry brought forth a myriad of bloody confrontations (to date I can claim seventy-three stitches), school was a distraction, dogs were always my best friends, and to this day I don't trust cats.

My grandfather was an ore miner in northern Minnesota and then became a banker, toiling under the truly evil eyes of a manager bent on demeaning the lowly likes of gentle men. Eventually gramps ran for and was elected mayor of his hometown. Nana had the patience of a statue, the mind of an educated diplomat, and the beauty of an Irish/Scandinavian doll. She kept gramps in line. They both drank, but his social interaction always seemed to push the lines of propriety after a few, and she would have to tether him in... A well-intentioned reminder of who was in charge.

My dad is a great guy and made some unique contributions to my development. He flew big planes in WWII, dropping paratroopers on D-Day, making loops between England and France for two tours. I still grill him for stories. My mom is a computer genius and a Life Master bridge player. She also paints, weaves and sculpts with glorious, artistic panache. But it was my dad's brother, Uncle Fred, who kick-started my interest in flight. He never saw combat action, but he flew *jets* — and I love jets.

The seed was sown. Off I went. Zipped through all the preliminaries of flight training, cut a swath to Top Gun, eventually found a home with Special Forces. It all came together in Special Forces — a sweet niche of naughty doings. Spent some time training the Norwegian SF contingent, with a sharp focus on mountain survival and commando tactics. It was fun, and I still stay in touch with a half dozen equally frostbitten individuals.

I can't talk about what I do these days professionally, but I spend a lot of time in Northern Minnesota, soaking up the spirit of my grand dad, and sniffing the pine-permeated air. I go fishing, but to this day, I have never caught one. λ

Dr Daniel Jackson

"Colonel O'Neill thinks I'm a geek. I have no idea how to get us back. I'll never get paid."

The task of re-inventing a character well known and loved from another medium has always been a bit of an uphill struggle, but it's one actor Michael Shanks approached with relish. Invited to re-create the role of Dr Daniel Jackson, the dedicated linguist and scientist left behind on the remote planet of Abydos at the end of the *Stargate* feature film, Shanks was delighted to be given the opportunity to make the character his own. Though he was briefed to get as close to the original characterisation as possible, Shanks states, "The producers also allowed me to incorporate my own subtleties and uniqueness into the portrayal." First reports confirmed that he played the young, passionate archaeologist and anthropologist to perfection. Shanks modestly suggests, "It was quite a challenging prospect, but the reaction from the audience was incredibly positive and supportive."

Shanks describes the character as "a dreamer. An ideologist who has a love of humanity and life in general. He's an eternal optimist, the kind of guy who is always looking for the best in people and situations." As lovely as it sounds, Daniel's philosophy has caused the SG-1 team some grief on occasion. In 'Need', his impulsive decision to prevent a king's daughter from throwing herself off a cliff sees the rest of his comrades up to their ears in Naquadah. And in 'Message in a Bottle', the orb Jackson insists is transported back to Earth bursts its shell, almost kills O'Neill, and puts the whole planet in peril!

"Daniel is always looking for answers," Shanks states. "He needs to know who we are, how we got here and why." This continual thirst for knowledge has led him into some dangerous places. In 'The Torment of Tantalus', Daniel is ready to risk everything, including his life, to find out more about the "meaning of Life stuff." The character is forced to walk a fine line between obsession and diligence while studying some mysterious alien records, which have been found after being lost for many years, and refuses to leave until it is almost too late. "I think that any archaeologist would be absolutely flabbergasted by the opportunity that Daniel is provided and would have to take it as far as he could," says Shanks of his character's actions in the episode.

Although it may appear that Dr Jackson is the one person totally against the use of force, who often steps in with a hopeful, "Hi! I'm

Daniel. We're peaceful explorers", Shanks insists the character "isn't exactly a pacifist. It's just that within the context of the Stargate Command Centre he's surrounded by military people, so he looks like one." For instance, when Daniel opts to help some primitive villagers deal with a manic despot in 'The First Commandment' it's because he genuinely wants to find a mutually beneficial situation. However, certain circumstances have forced him to take more forceful measures. In 'Within the Serpent's Grasp' he fires on the Goa'uld to buy more time for his colleagues. 'Bloodlines' sees the good Doctor wrestle with his conscience over whether or not to destroy a tank sustaining a clutch of infant Goa'uld. Blasting the tank, hence killing all but one of the larvae, Shanks explains, "Given the circumstances it's a very natural reaction. Daniel is angry at the bad guys for taking his wife, for enslaving people and realises that this is the only way to deal with them. It's not a decision he takes lightly."

Shanks' decision to pursue a career in acting wasn't a spur of the moment whim: "I started off doing Commercial Studies at university and then realised that all I really wanted to do was perform." Changing courses, he graduated with a Bachelor of Fine Arts degree from the University of British Columbia before being whisked off to the other side of Canada to work at the Stratford Shakespeare Festival in Ontario. Guest spots on television and in films soon followed. He made his film début in *Call of the Wild* and featured in series such as *The Commish*, *Highlander* and *The Outer Limits* before taking up his appointment with Dr Daniel Jackson. "I have a very short attention span," he grins, "so keep my hand in with other projects when not filming *Stargate SG-1*. I love the 'rush' you get when you perform on stage, so I played Hamlet for five weeks, and I've done a couple of independent movies." Two to look out for are *The Artist's Circle* and *Suspicious River*, both of which also include appearances by Don S. Davis.

An intensely private man off the set, Shanks tends to steer clear of the whole celebrity thing. Producer John Smith smiles, "Michael will usually be last on set, looking like he just got up three minutes before. He turns in a great day's work, then doesn't hang around."

The fact that the locals in Vancouver are used to the city being an extended film set, and see actors wandering around all the time, suits Shanks down to the ground. "People here are pretty blasé about all this star stuff, and don't really bother you. Fortunately, once I take off Daniel's glasses and hat I have the kind of looks that blend in with everybody else," Shanks admits. "I only tend to get recognised if I'm with the others, especially Christopher Judge. He walks around with Teal'c's tattoo on his forehead!" he jokes. His friend Judge laughs, "Shanks will soon have reached celebrity recluse status." The actor does sneak the odd look at fan websites, though he doesn't get involved in 'chats', offering, "It's not that I don't want to, I just prefer to hold on to a little bit of mystery."

Asked which personality traits he feels he shares with the character he plays, Shanks suggests, "There's a lot of me in Daniel. Daniel has a lot more curiosity, but I guess I would describe myself as stubborn, enthusiastic, genuine, naive and playful." Shanks feels the relationships between his character and the other members of SG–1 have deepened over the course of the series, allowing Daniel to become more of a team player. "I think there will always be that slight antagonism between Daniel and Jack, because of the very nature of their personalities," he says, adding, "his bond with Teal'c and Sam Carter is being allowed to develop, although I'd like to see more of that."

The friendships between the cast members have been close from day one: "I do play golf and ski with some of the cast and crew, but not nearly enough as I would like." A quiet but deadly joker on set, Shanks' impressions of characters from *The Simpsons* have caused his co-stars to 'corpse' on many occasions. Christopher Judge reveals that he is still thinking of ways to pay back the many practical jokes Shanks has played on him. "I'm too scared to tell you what they are," whispers Judge. "You don't know what he'll do to retaliate in the future!"

With regard to Daniel Jackson's future, Shanks is happy to leave that to the writers: "When we started out, we stayed close to the original characterisation, but then they followed my lead with regard to bringing Daniel more depth and scope to explore his darker side. I'm happy to wait to see what they come up with next. Like the audience, I just want to see what happens and enjoy the journey." Å

Major Sam Carter

"Colonel, I logged over 100 hours in enemy air space during the Gulf War. Is that tough enough for you? Or are we going to have to arm wrestle?"

When Sam Carter gives advice to SG-1, or indeed anyone at the Stargate Command Centre, it's usually based on some highly technical or scientific theory, and it invariably gets them out of a dire situation. With Amanda Tapping, you're more likely to get into trouble as a result of her words of wisdom. "You should never order Caesars [a vodka-based cocktail] from a Japanese restaurant," she nods, having told an innocent journalist to order the thing in the first place. Sam Carter would never order Daniel Jackson to drink something that would make his eyes water!

The mischievous Ms Tapping is worlds away from the rather sober Air Force ma'am seen in seasons one and two. Any of her colleagues will confirm the fact. "She's a comedienne in another life," explains Christopher Judge. "She knows exactly what to do or say — or even what *not* to do, to get me to laugh." Tapping protests that Judge has things the wrong way round, and that it's Judge and his cohorts that start her off. "It's usually at the end of the day," she says, "and it's usually my 'close-up', and the guys will all stand behind the camera trying to get me to crack up — which happens a lot. It happened just the other day when all five of us were in the briefing room. Rick was having trouble getting a line out, but wanted to keep the cameras rolling as he said he'd get it, but Michael and Christopher kept making little asides and gestures, and I started to laugh so much I had tears rolling down my cheeks. I kept thinking it was insane. There was no way they could use that footage. Eventually, they just lowered the camera covering me, and turned it off. I was a wreck!"

Starting off as a captain then progressing to major, Carter is the lynchpin of SG-1, the bridge between the military mind of Colonel O'Neill and the altruistic dreamer Dr Jackson. She's had to overcome many obstacles to prove her worth in the military, 'the biggest boys' club in the world'. Carter's immediate response to her superior's jibe — "Just because my reproductive organs are on the inside doesn't mean I can't handle whatever you can" — comes as a result of having to handle many such prejudices in her chosen career. But her strength, determination and sheer professionalism have won through, and brought her to the fore. "Sam is very strong, very smart and committed to the Stargate programme almost

to the point of obsession," Tapping explains. "For instance, Sam and Daniel can often be found working through the night to prove some theory or other."

Tapping feels the character has come a long way since her inception. "In the pilot, the writers had created this hard-assed feminist with a very didactic message, which I was really opposed to. But," she shrugs, "I really wanted to work on the show, so once I knew they were going to continue with the character, I approached the writers, who agreed we couldn't carry on with the gender argument. It was too boring."

By going with her own unique responses, Tapping feels she has managed to round Carter into a more fully developed personality. "I've tried to give Sam the toughness of a soldier without losing any of her femininity," the actress says, "although she's so dedicated to her job that it seems as though she has no life outside Stargate Command." Luckily, some 'life' comes to her: "Sam does have the hint of a burgeoning relationship with Narim in 'Enigma' and, of course, there's a *frisson* with Martouf in 'The Tok'ra'."

At work or play, Tapping's relations with those around her are cordial to say the least. Her warm nature and consummate professionalism are legendary. "All our cast are great," Jonathan Glassner smiles, "because we never once had to say we wouldn't write something because so-and-so wouldn't be able to play it, but that's especially the case with Amanda. She'd be given these long speeches, with all this technical jargon and 'protoplasmic blah', and it would come tripping off her tongue as though she had complete knowledge of what it meant!" In fact, Tapping *does* understand a lot of it. Swearing she's not a 'techno-geek' she concedes, "I like to know what I'm talking about, so I do research the technical and scientific stuff. I've learned a lot. Maybe not enough to get me a job... but then I have a great job."

"You know with Amanda that she's going to be the first on set," producer John Smith testifies. "She's going to be five minutes early with a big smile on her face, every day. Not only that, but she'll be fully prepared, and have her dialogue in place. She's got the lion's share and it's all that technobabble that she rattles off like nobody's business." Smith can't say enough about the actress's 'gung ho' approach, no matter what's thrown at her. "She's out there in the wind, the rain and the mud without a murmur. She's always a trouper."

It's hard to spare Ms Tapping's blushes with so many of her colleagues bursting to say how fantastic she is, but it's rare to meet a leading lady who

has yet to realise that she is one. The
gang in the make-up trailer is clearly
besotted. "We call the first shot and the
last shot of the day Amanda shots," says
make-up supervisor Jan Newman,
"because she's the one we have to get
ready first and she's usually the last to
leave. She's as bright at the end of the
day as when she arrives." Newman
repeats a quote she's used before, but
claims Tapping has never altered in the
time she's been associated with her:
"Amanda has that high star quality without the star attitude. She's very special."
The make-up supervisor admits to having a very soft spot for the actress, just
because "she's the girl. It's like a moth-
er/daughter thing. Amanda can be too
accommodating sometimes, and will
carry on doing whatever is asked of her
till she drops. I've given her several

books on how to say 'no' but I'm not sure she's read them yet!"

Peter Williams has this to say: "Most of my relations on set are
with Amanda, and I find her a very genuine person. She doesn't really 'dig' the star thing, but finds herself in a place where she needs to
be a little bit conscious of it because of the popularity of the show."

Insisting that the experience makes her feel humble, Tapping
regards her growing popularity as a source of pleasure which she
shares with the fans. Although she left England for the States when
just a child, Tapping is proud of her Rochford roots and has delighted the British contingent by teasing that she's bought some white
stiletto shoes and has learned to dance round her handbag in the best
'Essex-girl' tradition.

Whilst *Stargate SG-1* is the vehicle which has propelled Tapping to
international recognition, she's not a newcomer to stage or screen. Since
graduating from the University of Windsor School of Dramatic Art, she has
appeared in numerous theatre productions including *Steel Magnolias* and
Noises Off. A host of small screen credits include *The X-Files*, *Due South*,
Forever Night and *The Outer Limits*. Her latest big screen role is as the leading lady in *The Void*, due to be released in late 2001. ⋏

Teal'c

"In my world, I would be well within my rights to dismember you."

Habitually late, prone to fits of giggling and a firm believer that bashing a little ball about with a metal pole is a commendable sport (he's a keen golfer) — Christopher Judge possesses more than a few personal foibles the sombre Teal'c would find hard to understand. As chief protector and second in command to the System Lord Apophis, the stoic Jaffa executed many difficult and unpleasant tasks, not to mention executing innocent aliens into the bargain. Judge says that in real life it's his colleagues who have to display fortitude and patience. "To tell you the truth, I don't know how the guys at SG-1 put up with me," he laughs. Fortunately, the actor's co-stars and colleagues cope remarkably well. Make-up supervisor Jan Newman describes Judge as the bane of her life, yet the normally genteel lady chuckles, "I have no compunction about shouting like a fishwife when he's kept us waiting. But he is so adorable that he can be an hour late and within three seconds I've forgiven him." Judge thinks it's a pity Apophis doesn't feel the same way. Producer John Smith grins, "Christopher will *eventually* come in with a big smile on his face and push everybody — in a very gentle way, not hard enough to knock us over as he's a big guy — but it tickles him to do it and it makes us laugh."

However, the actor maintains it's everyone else that keeps *him* laughing, protesting, "Amanda Tapping can break my composure with one look." Judge's exuberance extends to the other members of the cast, particularly Michael Shanks with whom he has forged a firm friendship. "I'm always teasing Shanks about the way he prepares for every scene," laughs Judge. "Me? I just ask him if I need to read the script."

Speaking socially as well as professionally, Judge claims, "Shanks and I are as different as chalk and cheese. He's a quiet, country boy at heart and I'm a city slicker, but we gelled straight off and have stayed that way." As well as joining the other sporty cast members in a love of skiing, Judge says Michael Shanks and Richard Dean Anderson share his fascination with golf. In a fit of uncharacteristic modesty he admits, "I'm not as good as they are yet, but I'm working on it. In fact, if I'm not hanging out on the set or spending time with my kids, you'll most likely find me practising my swing on the golf course."

Not that it's all play and no work for the ex-First Prime of Apophis, Serpent God. Since his initial stiff-upper-lip appearances, SG-1's tower of strength and authority on all things Goa'uld has been loosening up a little. "I spoke with the writers about how Teal'c was starting to assimilate, and brought it to their attention that he has a great sense of humour," Judge recalls. "It's just different from a human sense of humour. I wanted to make a conscious effort to get Teal'c to make what he thought were jokes and to bring out the human characteristics he has that had so far been dormant in the show." Teal'c's slant on the 'wild horses couldn't drag me away' promise in 'Message in a Bottle' being a prime example. In the episode, an alien device grows robotic legs and pins SG-1's team leader to the

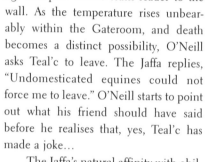

wall. As the temperature rises unbearably within the Gateroom, and death becomes a distinct possibility, O'Neill asks Teal'c to leave. The Jaffa replies, "Undomesticated equines could not force me to leave." O'Neill starts to point out what his friend should have said before he realises that, yes, Teal'c has made a joke...

The Jaffa's natural affinity with children comes to the fore particularly in 'Bane', when he rewards his young saviour Ally by presenting her with a bigger, more powerful, but less than lethal version of a staff weapon. Teal'c's growing affection for and understanding of Daniel Jackson is displayed too, when he soaks him with the aforementioned water pistol, before dashing off in wild pursuit of the youngster.

Christopher Judge was born and raised in Los Angeles where, he jokes, "the closest I came to any wild life was in the bars." The jovial ex-All American footballer was drawn to acting from an early age. "I studied Telecommunications and Film at the University of Oregon, and knew I was destined to be in the spotlight," he says. Judge's 'break' came when he won a competition, which earned him a job as morning DJ on a West Coast radio station. From there it was a hop, skip and a jump to television, where he appeared in *The Fresh Prince of Bel Air* and *21 Jump Street* (alongside Peter DeLuise). As well as appearing in a wealth of motion pictures, including *Bird on a Wire* with Mel Gibson and Goldie Hawn and *House Party II*, Judge also cut his teeth behind the scenes when he produced a short film entitled *Hacks*, a career extension he intends to pursue alongside his *Stargate SG-1* stint. Known amongst his friends as "the Barry White of SG-1" Judge has recently recorded a CD featuring many of his favourite types of musical styles. "Christopher has a beautiful voice. He has a wonderful range and is incredibly smooth," enthuses Jan Newman. She should know, as she's married to a singer!

A man of many talents, Judge has been known to wax lyrical about the role of black actors in mainstream productions. "When I initially glanced at the script for *Stargate SG-1*, I thought this was going to be yet another example of where the big, tough, black guy is your stereotyped reformed slave," he recalls. "But when I read it properly, I realised that here was a chance to let 'the guy with the muscle' be the one who might just lead his people from slavery — that there was a nobility in him." Catching himself, Judge goes on, "Of course, he can't do that without some sex. That's one of the reasons Teal'c doesn't smile so much. His wife is hidden on another planet!"

Talking with Judge is akin to riding a rollercoaster. He can be as deep and serious as they come one moment, ridiculously silly the next. It's a notion the actor is keen to foster in his performance of the quiet Jaffa. "As a character I didn't have a lot to say in the beginning, which I felt was in keeping with how he was meant to be," he says. "My reactions as Teal'c were more honest in that they were pertinent to an intelligent man who finds himself in an unfamiliar environment on an unknown world. As the series progresses and Teal'c does speak, it's because he really has something to say worth hearing. He's more interactive with his companions and in tune with those around him."

Christopher Judge is also 'in tune' with the world around him, and is actively involved raising awareness of and funds for the Boys and Girls Club of Canada. A committed family man who often brings his three children to set so they can spend more time together, he feels every effort should be made to support and sustain kids the world over. As he so eloquently puts it, "What can be more important than our children?" ⅄

General Hammond

"He's a very good, very bald man from Texas."

Don S. Davis is the embodiment of General George Hammond. Born and raised in the Missouri mountains, he remains a country boy at heart. When several injuries curtailed his football career in college, Davis stayed on to study theatre. Having spent three years in the army — "I was a captain during the Vietnam period," he says, "and though I was never stationed there I did serve in Korea. It was good experience for me" — Davis decided to return to his theatrical roots. He gained a Masters and a Doctorate in theatre studies and taught at Southern Illinois University. "The acting part came much later," he grins, "I was a late bloomer. I didn't take this up till I was in my forties." Ironically, he got his first break as stand-in for Dana Eclar, the actor who played *MacGyver*'s boss. A veteran of over thirty films and television shows (including acclaimed performances in *Twin Peaks* and *The X-Files*), Davis is also an admired painter, sculptor and wood carver.

Here's what Don S. Davis has to say about his current *alter ego*:

Thoughts on General Hammond
By Don S. Davis

I don't really know what to tell you about General Hammond other than he's a character that I enjoy playing. I think that as a young officer, he was a man who liked pushing himself to his limits, who enjoyed a bit of danger. It may be that that aspect of his character is what has made him so predisposed to overlook O'Neill's shenanigans. He admires Jack's courage, and his willingness to go to the limit in fighting for something he believes in.

The Air Force motto is 'integrity first, service before self and excellence in all we do'. One of the things I have tried to show throughout the filming of this series is that George Hammond is a man of great integrity, his word is his bond. He holds duty and honour in utmost regard. He is not going to betray his country or his troops if he can help it, no matter what. He may have to accept that, at times, people in his position in other divisions of the American armed forces might do things that are morally questionable or of questionable honour and integrity, but he doesn't like it. By nature he is a man who believes in doing the right thing at all times.

As for 'service before self', he actually resigned in one episode

when his family was threatened because he couldn't compromise them, and he knew that he couldn't put himself and his family's interests above his duties and the needs of his country in command decisions. He felt he had no alternative, he couldn't betray his duty to his country, even for the welfare of his family.

And 'excellence in all we do'? Well, he expects his troops to do the best job they possibly can in any situation, and he tries to do the best job he can in every situation. He would be deeply offended by somebody in his command taking a slipshod or a lackadaisical attitude in performing their duties. He is a man who demands excellence from all of those whom he serves with.

I think Hammond loves his job. In the first episode he says to O'Neill, "I took this job so that I'd have an easy assignment that would allow me to look back over my career and work on my memoirs." Obviously he's had some kind of an exciting career or he wouldn't think that it warranted memoirs.

He's angry that Apophis came through the Stargate and attacked his base. He was initially angry with O'Neill, because he suspected that something about this man's initial reports was not true, or this wouldn't have happened. However, in the very first encounter, when O'Neill and his team go off, Hammond is shrewd enough to see that they are good people, and he dedicates himself to helping them get this job done for as long as it takes. I think he's a good guy. His wife has died, though he still wears his wedding band so he must have had a great love. He's got some grandkids that are the apple of his eye, he loves them so much that he is willing to step down rather than have them used as his Achilles heel.

As I've said in many interviews, if there is anything I'd like to see revealed about Hammond, it would be something of his private life that shows his passions. However, that's not what the series is about, so I'm not sure that's even appropriate within the grand scheme of things. ⋋

Hammond's Guide to Leadership

Leadership is the ability to influence the direction, goals and efforts of others through means that include, but go beyond, the simple exercise of authority.

A leader always challenges his men to do their best to get the job done. He sets a good example for them to follow. If an officer is delegating authority, he should help the men to whom he's delegating to polish their thoughts. He should make sure they understand everything clearly; make sure that they know how to get the job done before they present those orders to the people under them.

It's important that a commander's men know he has their best interests at heart, and that he is going to do everything he can to help them succeed. A good leader makes sure his men get the credit for a job well done.

If there's a reason that something can't be done, if the ability to complete the job has for some reason been taken out of their hands, don't punish them, stand by them, back them to the hilt. If you give someone orders, and they come back to you with a concern or a report, make sure you listen hard to what they say. Whether it's reporting a success or failure, listen well, and retain what you've been told.

If you make a promise to your people, just as in life when you make a promise to anyone whom you care about, make sure you keep that promise unless it's humanly impossible to do so.

Don't assume a mantle of arrogance and if you're wrong, admit it. You have to be available to listen, and be easy to talk to, not difficult.

One of the jobs of the man in charge is to keep his troops focussed on the goals ahead. Every military mission involves the selection and maintenance of a particular aim. It's your job to keep your men informed, and on course.

When a mission fails and someone of an equal, or lesser rank has gone against your recommendations, don't jump on them with an 'I told you so.' However, don't be bashful about pointing out why, if they had done another thing, the job might have gone better. Don't hold it over them, don't play God and make them feel small. Be honest and be positive in your criticisms. If somebody does something wrong, unless it's imperative that you correct them on the spot at that moment, do your correcting in private. Regardless of how they try to mask their feelings, no one likes to be humiliated in public. Always try to be honest in your conduct and your statements, and be courageous. If you have to stand there and take a shot, take the shot.

There is a lot of stress in any kind of military endeavour because there are always high stakes. It's vital in leadership to know your own strengths and weaknesses: what you can and can't do. You have to be willing, at times, to grin and bear it, or just laugh it off and walk away. A sense of humour in any situation in life, and especially in a situation dealing with the military, is absolutely essential. (As told to Don S. Davis.)

Recurring characters

Brad Wright

"From the very beginning our aim has been to try to incorporate new characters into the mix."

Teryl Rothery is bright, bubbly and vivacious, totally unlike her SG-1 persona, **Dr Janet Fraiser**. "Brad and I had worked with Teryl on a number of occasions," says executive producer Jonathan Glassner, "and it didn't take a lot of thought on our part to sign her up." The actress couldn't be more thrilled that they did: "I went from a one episode guest appearance, to recurring, to regular cast member and thank my lucky stars daily for the privilege."

Having started her career at the tender age of thirteen dancing in a musical production of *Bye Bye Birdie*, Rothery has honed her skills in every area of the profession. Among her stage appearances was an award-winning performance in *Annie Get Your Gun*, and she has featured in many television shows, such as *The X-Files* and *The Outer Limits*. Film credits include *Masterminds* with her all time hero, Patrick Stewart. "I could just sit and listen to him reading the phone book," she sighs. She also works on voiceovers for animation, most notably the universally acclaimed *Noddy* series. "I don't have a preference for any particular medium," she says, "I just feel the need to continually stretch myself and deepen my performance, whatever the context."

Within the precepts of *Stargate SG-1*, Dr Fraiser is cool, calm, collected and not the least bit scared of stepping into the fray. As Rothery puts it, remembering a particularly action-packed first season episode, "The girls kicked major butt in 'Hathor'!" Nor is Fraiser afraid of countermanding a higher-ranking officer. "She really did have the welfare of Colonel O'Neill, Sam and Teal'c as her main priority when she remonstrated with General Hammond in 'Fire and Water'," Rothery recalls. In reality, the actress claims that she is more likely to stand back and let a professional take care of any emergency situation. However, this was disproved at the recent *Gatecon* fan convention in Vancouver, when she was the first one to rush to a lady's aid when a glass of wine was spilled over her front. "It's OK, I'm a doctor!" she yelled as she expertly threw a glass of water over the woman's chest, whilst ordering another twenty-five centilitres of red to be injected into the nearest receptacle — "It was for medicinal purposes only, you understand."

A good friend of colleague Amanda Tapping, they share more than the responsibility of adopted ward Cassandra on the show. They both

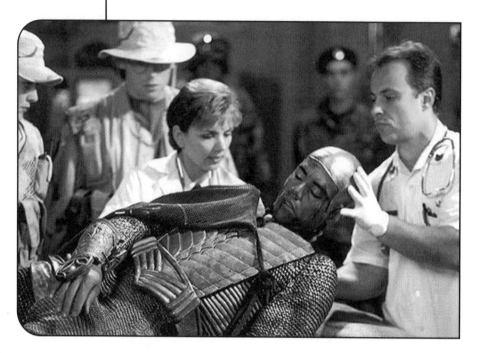

enjoy 'acting' off screen as well as on, it seems. "Amanda and I have this 'thing' going where we pretend to be two Southern Belles at beauty school," Rothery explains. "I'm 'Charlene' and Amanda is 'Minnie'!" The women are also totally in tune with their pets: "Amanda got herself the cutest little dog. Well, it's actually the size of a house. So I thought, I'll go and get me one too." Rothery is happy to report that mother and puppy are doing well. In fact, there's nothing she likes more on dark and rainy Vancouver days than settling down with a blanket and Bodie to read a good book.

Here are Teryl Rothery's thoughts on a character very dear to her heart:

Dr Janet Fraiser
By Teryl Rothery

When I first appeared on *Stargate SG-1* it was to guest star as a doctor. A doctor by the name of Fraiser. It was to be a one-time thing with the *possibility* of it turning into what is called a recurring role. Well, as I write this we are now into our fifth season and Dr Fraiser is a regular. She even has a first name… Janet. Now, because the show was never really written with her in mind as a regular, I was given no background on her. No history. I learned about Janet the same way you did… with each new episode she was written into. Each and every actor creates a character his or her own way. I personally like to know their history. I feel the only way to get into their skin, is to know them inside out. Therefore, I created *my own* background for her. You may not agree with it. In fact, you may have created a far more exciting history for her. If so, let's talk (just kidding!). Anyway, this is the Janet that I know…

She is the eldest of three children and has two brothers. Their names are Scott Jameson Fraiser and Jeffrey Sutton Fraiser. Her full name by the way is Janet Elizabeth Fraiser. Her father is a retired army officer, her mother a homemaker who would sew, do alterations and knit to bring in extra money. Not to mention keep her sane. Her parents' names are Jameson Franklin and Marjorie Kathryn Fraiser. Her mother's maiden name was Sutton.

Marjorie (although her friends and family call her 'Kate') is a very warm, fun-loving spirit. She has a wonderful sense of humour, which she has passed on to her children. Yes, as contained as Janet is, she does have a wicked sense of humour, you just don't get the chance to see it. There has been the odd occasion where you've been allowed to see snippets of it. I call her the iceberg because her core, her true essence is kept covered up. For the most part you only get to see what's on the surface.

She's an awful lot like her father. He too is very contained. He would never be accused of wearing his heart on his sleeve, if you get my drift. He also errs on the side of chauvinism, although it really is too strong a word to describe him. Janet has always felt she's had to seek his approval. She pushes herself to please him, not only joining the Air Force (he was hoping it would be the army) but going through medical school and then specialising in exotic diseases. The thing is, he is extremely proud of her; he just doesn't know how to show it. Consequently, she keeps driving herself.

The best thing that ever happened to her was Cassandra. Okay, it was the second best thing. The first was getting rid of that pompous, chauvinistic husband she was married to. Fortunately it only lasted three years. Three very *long* years!! Anyway, I digress. Cassie has given her life balance. I really think having Cassie has allowed her to 'open up' somewhat. I think it's the first time Janet has really given herself permission to love.

Well… I hope you enjoyed my version of Janet. I know that there is so much more to her and I would love to go deeper, share a little more with you, but for that I guess you'll just have to keep tuning in to *Stargate SG-1*…

Apophis, Serpent God Ruler of the Night, doesn't appear to have a single saving grace: he takes from the poor, kills off the rich, infests innocent aliens with his ill-gotten larvae and is downright rotten to the members of SG-1. Cue chorus of reptilian-type noises. The actor who plays the slippery snake, the divine Peter Williams, thinks the whole thing is a hoot! "What I've learned from this character," he drawls, "is that I have a mean streak so wide you wouldn't believe it. As Apophis it's great to give it some release. I actually find pleasure in tormenting Daniel Jackson and the rest of his miserable compatriots." But how about looking at a gentler side of SG-1's nemesis? Shaking his head, Williams sighs, "I'm not sure there is a gentler side to Apophis but *I'm* the total opposite." The actor feels this is partly due to his Jamaican heritage. He was born and raised there, then moved to England for six years before re-locating to Toronto. Although he's lived in different places, he still retains the softest of Jamaican brogues. Williams's striking good looks made him a prime target for talent agents, and many photographic assignments were pushed his way, although modelling soon lost its charm: "It wasn't stimulating enough so I moved on to the performing

THINGS TO REMEMBER TO PACK ON MY NEXT MISSION

By Apophis — Serpent God Ruler of the Night (as told to Peter Williams).

1. Treats for the kids
2. Megaphone — easier on the voice
3. 'Harem' of female attendants
4. Goa'uld wrist/palm device and forcefield
5. Visine eye drops
6. Miniature Teal'c/O'Neill dolls to stick pins into
7. Extra gold lipstick and eyeliner — just in case
8. Vocume walkman proposal for the Sony people
9. Track #6 on the Children of the Gods CD
10. Guestbook for fans to sign

OH YEAH! Almost forgot!! A SARCOPHAGUS!!!

Apophis doesn't play by the rules — he gets to have 11 on a Top 10 list.

arts." The actor's television credits include *MacGyver* and *Neon Rider* (for which Brad Wright was one of the writers). Ironically, the pilot episode of *Stargate* saw Williams faced by reminders of his former profession: "'Children of the Gods' will always live on in my memory because all the Goa'ulds they hired as extra cast members were models. So we were surrounded by these beautiful men and women."

To date the actor has appeared in more than twenty films, including *Soul Survivor*, which was written and directed by his brother Stephen. One of his latest projects, *Love Come Down*, in which he stars as an abusive father, was nominated for nine Genie awards — one of Canada's most prestigious recognitions of excellence. Given his loving personality, Williams admits, "It was quite a stretch for me but it was a sweet, sweet part to get. I had to beat a lot of American talent to get it."

Williams has no such difficulty flexing his muscles in *Stargate* and loves the way his relationship with SG-1 has built up over the years: "From Daniel and O'Neill there's a natural antagonism, which I can understand, given the circumstances. Teal'c is just a lackey and gofer. I want to get rid of him altogether. As for Samantha — I'm not supposed to like anyone so don't quote me, but — in Goa'uld, we'd say, 'She's fine.'"

Although Apophis has reputedly bitten the dust more than once, the writers consider him too good a villain to kill off completely — which is heaven-sent news for his millions of worshippers across the globe. Bad news for the good guys of SG-1 though!

Tony Amendola plays **Bra'tac**, a rogue Jaffa Master, and friend and mentor to Teal'c, who has been known to teach Jack O'Neill a few lessons in his time. Between wrestling him to the ground in 'Bloodlines', bashing him on the nose in 'Within the Serpent's Grasp' and leading him into the lion's den in 'Family', even the character exclaims, "Not bad for an old'un."

Amendola remembers the day he received the 'break down' of the character: "It says he is 133 years old and I thought, 'Do I want to sit in make-up for three hours?' Well, on the first day, the make-up lady looks at me and says, 'OK — nothing needed here.' I didn't know how to feel about that!"

A veteran of performance, Amendola lists *The Mask of Zorro*, *Nowhere Man*, *Seinfeld*, *Ally McBeal* and *The Visitor* amongst his many film and television appearances.

The beautiful Abydan wife of Daniel Jackson, **Sha're** is kidnapped by Teal'c and forced to share her body with Apophis's mate Ammonet. The original focus of the young archaeologist is to trace his bride and try to restore her to the woman she once was. Sadly, his plans go slightly awry when he finds her a year later only to discover she is pregnant with Apophis's child. Tahitian beauty queen and actress Vaitiare Bandera, who counts *US Marshals* amongst her screen appearances, was actually expecting a baby during the filming of the 'Secrets' episode. Peter Williams is *not* the father!

Bronx boy Alexis Cruz plays **Skaara**, friend of Jack O'Neill and brother to Sha're. Kidnapped by serpent guards, he is forced to host a Goa'uld larvae and become the adopted son of Apophis. If Daniel Jackson's quest

is to find his wife, Jack O'Neill's pledge to bring Skaara back to the fold is just as irrefutable. A firm favourite on *Stargate SG-1*, Cruz has also graced the screens in *NYPD Blue*, *E.R.* and *Touched by an Angel.*

General Jacob Carter is immensely proud of his estranged daughter Samantha, and knows that if only she got her head out of a computer and into the clouds she would make a first class astronaut. His delight when he finds out that she already goes far beyond the realms any such traveller could dream of is tempered only by the knowledge that he discovers this at a point where a terrible cancer seems poised to take his life. Fortunately, Sam's explorations lead him to a place where he can either choose to live the rest of his days as a Tok'ra host, thereby fulfilling his ambition to serve the people of Earth and enjoy a long and healthy life occasionally shared by his child, or die. Jacob chooses life.

Based in Los Angeles, actor Carmen Argenziano has more than one hundred screen appearances to his credit, including roles in *Gone in Sixty Seconds*, *Hellraiser: Inferno*, *Ties That Bind* and *Party of Five.* ⅄

SG-1 Travel Essentials

Stargate:

A transportation device which links together a vast network of planets across more than one galaxy. Made by a race known as The Ancients, the first Earth Stargate was discovered in 1928. Stargates operate by entering a code of seven chevrons — six of which specify the position of the 'receiving' Gate, with the seventh designating the point of origin or 'sending' Gate. The device works by opening a stable wormhole between two gates. Anything or anyone moving into the watery portal, also known as 'the puddle', that forms across the Gate is immediately broken down into component molecules, compressed, then reconstituted at the other end. The Gate's operation is usually accompanied by a loud 'kawoosh' sound.

Dial Home Device (DHD):

Stargates are usually operated by a DHD, although various homemade contraptions have sufficed on occasion. Similar to the dial on a primitive telephone, the DHD contains all the 'numbers' needed to 'call' a particular address. The thirty-nine 'glyphs' correspond to the ones around the Stargate. Once the number has been punched in, a large red dome at the centre of the device is pushed to activate the programme.

Remote Identification Device (RID):

This hand-held dohickey — to give its technical term — allows in-coming travellers to let the folks back home know they are Earth-friendly. In order to stop unwanted visitors from breezing in through the Gate, a specially reinforced titanium iris was put in place. The almost impenetrable screen is less than three micrometers from the event horizon of the wormhole and could cause substantial physical damage to anyone or anything bumping into it. A few trusted individuals, such as Bra'tac, some Tok'ra and Thor's buddies have been given their own RID to enable them to visit or send messages to the Tau'ri when they want to.

Personnel's Personal Preferences (PPPs):

Non-essential but nice to have along.

O'Neill — Fishing pole. No fish required, it's the fishing that counts.

Carter — *Zen and the Art of Motorcycle Maintenance*. Simpler than building a DHD.

Jackson — Tissues. Much better than wiping hands on clothes.

Teal'c — Candles. The better to facilitate getting in touch with your true self.

Production Design

Richard Hudolin

"On most television shows, it's all about offices and police cars. On this show we don't do offices — we do worlds."

Asked where he gets the inspiration to create the award-winning designs for *Stargate SG-1*, production design master Richard Hudolin shrugs and says, "It's what we do! The writers present us with a situation and we come up with a look, or a feel, or a style. Then we make sure we know how to do it, and that we have the right people to get it done. I have a first class crew and know that any one of them can deliver the product without me having to worry about it." Insisting that the process is a collaborative affair, Hudolin wholeheartedly endorses the efforts of his team: "We have seven people in the art department, headed up by Bridget McGuire. Thom Wells heads construction, then there's the set decorators and props people all involved in making it happen. I do assign specific tasks, but we have an open art department so we all take a look at what other people are up to and help each other. Often people from other parts of production will wander in and offer their comments. Its one of the things I love about this job."

Hudolin claims he never gets nervous because there is simply no time. "I get the themes for ten shows well in advance," he explains, "so I'm working on this way ahead of everyone else." By the time an episode is actually being shot, Hudolin has long moved on, and is deep in preparation for the next batch. "If I go on set when they're shooting, I don't know what the heck is going on!" he laughs, but the designer maintains that employing a selective memory is one of the tools that keeps his mind fresh for the next project. "As soon as the shooting crew gets there I totally erase everything about that show from my mind. I can't remember a thing unless someone tells me what sets were involved. I just know that everything we do is great, and that's good enough for me." When pushed, Hudolin does consider 'The Nox', 'Spirits', 'Show and Tell', 'Thor's Chariot' and 'Family' as some of the most memorable episodes from the first two seasons. "You know, we won a Gemini award," he says proudly, "but when I was first asked to put an episode in for consideration, I had to look at the tapes to decide which one to nominate because it all becomes such a blur." Defending his amnesia, he grins, "I couldn't look to the future if I kept looking back at the others."

Opposite page: Concept drawings for the Death Glider (top) and the Hangar Bay with Gliders ready for action (bottom). Page 134: Production design art for the Castle in 'Torment of Tantalus' (top) and Drey'ac and Fro'tak's home in 'Family' (bottom).

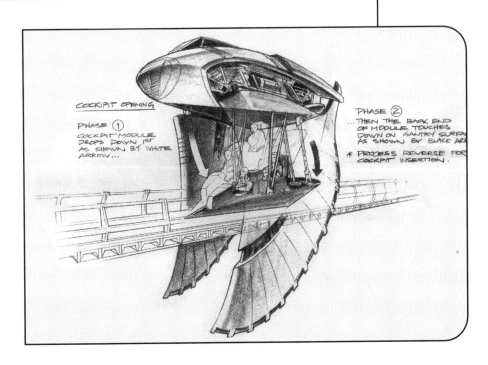

COCKPIT OPENING

PHASE ①

COCKPIT MODULE
DROPS DOWN 1ST
AS SHOWN BY WHITE
ARROW...

PHASE ②

...THEN THE BACK END
OF MODULE TOUCHES
DOWN ON GANTRY SURFA[CE]
AS SHOWN BY BLACK AR[ROW]

* PROCESS REVERSE FOR
COCKPIT INSERTION.

Page 135: Production design art for the Nox's Cloud City (top) and the meeting house from 'Spirits' (bottom). *Above: The portable Stargate on location.* *Opposite page: Preparing a shot with the Asgard in the studio.*

Whilst there may be the odd blooper (not many, we're assured) that occurs when an episode is being shot, Hudolin is adamant that no such thing ever happens during the design and construction process, teasing, "There's been none that I'm going to tell you about! Actually, because we move so quickly, you have to pick up potential errors straight away. I'll be walking by a set and if I don't catch something when somebody is starting to do it, it can lead to some pretty ugly pieces of work. They all laugh at me because I have this thing about rocks. Making rocks and caves is really difficult and you have to work at it and think about what you're doing, but every now and then I'll get on this rant and I'll be walking by a set and go, 'What the hell is that cartoon rock? Are the Flintstones working here?' The crew just watch me light up. Sometimes they do it deliberately just to get me riled. They enjoy watching me rant." It must be because raised voices are such an unusual occurrence. "You don't get much of that on our set," Hudolin confirms. "It doesn't achieve anything. No one on our set would pay attention anyway."

Boulders aside, there is one piece of construction of which Hudolin is extremely proud. "We have a portable Stargate, which we take on location.

It's an exact copy of the one in the studio, except the inner ring doesn't move. It takes six guys about a day to set it up because it has to be done in a very specific way, but it's a beautiful piece of engineering."

This engineering skill came to the fore many times during season one. "That year it rained till about June and we'd go on location and have to build roads because the trucks would sink into the ground," Hudolin recalls. Things were a lot more palatable for the crew in season two, however. "That was a great year, because we had established our rhythm and our systems of how we would do the show, and everybody knew what their function was going to be. That made it all great fun." Λ

Visual Effects

Joel Goldsmith, composer

"We have a terrific visual effects department. Often I try to imagine how grandiose and spectacular an effect will be and they always exceed my expectations and imagination."

Whenever you watch *Stargate SG-1* and hear a whiz or bang, witness an explosion or the mighty morphing military, spare a thought for the hard-working special visual effects teams beavering away with their pyrotechnics and computers blazing.

Innovative visual effects supervisor John Gajdecki is thrilled to have taken the opportunity to blow up the bad guys on this award-winning television show, although he took a bit of persuading at the start. "I had been working with the executive producers Brad Wright and Jonathan Glassner on *The Outer Limits*, but had decided to move on to pastures new," he remembers. "Brad and Jon kept phoning saying, 'C'mon we've got this great new thing going. Come on and do it!' However, I had other plans, which included going off and making movies, until I met one of the producers, Jeff King, at an awards ceremony. He reminded me that it was very rare to work on a show where everyone is your friend, so I decided to take a year out of my life and come work on *Stargate SG-1*. It turned out pretty well."

Gajdecki is president of GVFX, Canada's largest full-service visual effects company for the film and television industry. An amalgamation of multi-talented artists based in Toronto and Vancouver, the company's motto could well be 'collaboration in all things', as each department, from the model-makers, through motion control photography specialists to the compositors, greets the achievements of other colleagues as enthusiastically as its own. This attitude carries on through GVFX's work on *Stargate SG-1*. Gajdecki was visual effects supervisor on seasons one and two of the show. James Tichenor worked as his assistant on the first season, then moved into full-time supervision and has since become the visual effects producer for the entire series. Tichenor explains, "The way *Stargate* works is we have alternating supervisors, 'A' and 'B', working with co-ordinators. Initially it was John Gajdecki and I on 'B' and a number of different supervisors on 'A' rotation. Then, in season two, John became 'A' rotation supervisor with Simon Lacey and I became the man in charge of 'B' rotation." Confused? Don't be, it's done to prevent one team being responsible for all the major effects, which in turn keeps everything fresh and innovative. Tichenor feels the system works very well: "It's like I'm watching a new

Above: Filming the 'Kawoosh' effect, with the help of a water tank and an air cannon.

show when I see the episodes that the other team work on. I'm watching the same characters, but because I didn't get to read the script or spend a lot of time working through scenes bit by bit, it's a good surprise. When I get to look at the other guys' effects it's great because it's like, 'How did they do that?'" Tichenor does protest, though, that Gajdecki is like a master magician who always keeps his secrets to himself.

The award-winning team of Gajdecki, Ted Rae and Robert Habros created the effects for the pilot episode 'Children of the Gods'. Tichenor explains how his colleagues designed the infamous 'Kawoosh' effect of the Stargate in operation. "It's such a dynamic turbulent effect it's almost impossible for us to build in CG [Computer Generation]," he reveals. "We have tried to do it a couple of times, because we wanted to do more with it, and have different camera angles and what have you, but it never turns out quite as realistic. What we actually did to shoot the 'Kawoosh' was prepare a tank of water, modelled on what they did to create the effect in the feature film, and blast it with a little air cannon. The high-powered air mover had a very focussed nozzle exhorting major pounds per square inch of air into a very, very small point. We set that up in the water tank, and used gravity to our benefit. We shot the air cannon down and placed the camera shooting straight up at one hundred and twenty frames per second.

So we got the effect of this funnel of water coming straight through.

"The whole shot took about three days to film," Tichenor continues. "Working in GVFX's model shop in Toronto, they knew exactly which angles they needed, took the camera down, made the environment as black as possible and just started shooting. They ended up with about ten different angles, which we still use to this day. Every time we need a 'Kawoosh' in an episode we refer back to the ones we shot almost five years ago. We composite them into new shots and always have to very carefully match the perspective angles, so it takes a bit of time to get right."

According to Tichenor, all the members of the effects team have their favourite 'Kawoosh'. "There's quite a few to choose from. There's the side angle one where you really see the effect, or the one that goes straight at the camera. It's great to see that the effect works for different people on lots of different levels." Co-executive producer Robert Cooper agrees, "Sometimes fans get used to seeing how the Stargate operates, but it is pretty spectacular. It's great to watch new cast members' reactions to it. Carmen Argenziano [Jacob Carter] had never seen it in place before and kept saying, 'Wow! It's unbelievable!' when he saw the finished episode."

'The Torment of Tantalus' was the second episode that Robert Cooper wrote and featured a wealth of special effects never previously attempted on *Stargate*. The team had to create a Stargate effect and make it look like it was shot on film back in the 1940s. The blend between watching the scene on a monitor with Daniel and O'Neill, and the change to the archive footage was done so smoothly, that the effect is one of James Tichenor's favourites: "It was a dissolve from the 'real' shot that was done in the show, cut into the shot on the monitor on what we call 'play-back', and the two were just lined up.

"It was a treat to make the sequence black and white. We de-saturated all of the colours and did a sepia tone treatment to the whole shot after putting in the Stargate effect. We also added all of the scratches; the little bumps and grinds and all of the wrinkles you see on the film in the monitor. The other nice thing for me is that by taking out all the colour, I think it makes the Stargate pass-through work even better. It's the best one we've ever done in my opinion. It really does look like the character is walking through water."

Needless to say, these things take time, but such was the enthusiasm of Tichenor and his colleague Christine Petrov that they completed the effect over one weekend. "We shot all the stuff on set on the Friday, then Christine and I worked so they could have it back for the Monday morning. Nowadays, we could do it quickly, no problem, but back then, when the Stargate was a relatively new effect, we were still trying to figure out how to do it, so it was quite a challenge."

The effects for the superlative 'Serpent's Lair' were achieved using entirely different techniques. Describing the steps used to create the exploding Goa'uld motherships at the climax of the episode, Tichenor begins, "That was all a model shoot. John [Gajdecki] has a nifty setup in Toronto, where he has all the computers upstairs, but downstairs he has a fantastic model shop. That makes his company quite unique. Until about ten years ago, visual effects were all about models and building practical pieces that were cleverly lit, filmed and magically transformed into something they weren't. You have all the more power with a computer to enhance that, and John is able to do both."

Indulging his passion for blowing things to smithereens, Gajdecki enthusiastically recalls, "The exploding motherships were great fun to shoot. They were twenty feet wide, and filled with explosives and debris." The effect is achieved with a combination of practical devices and CG effects. "When we want to blow things up, we don't actually build the whole model with all the detailing and finish that you see on screen,"

Above: Preparing to blow up a model Goa'uld mothership for the climax of 'Serpent's Lair'.

Gajdecki explains, "but construct what's called a 'black box', that has the shape and dimensions we want. Then we apply the textures and detailing using computers. But when we blow up the models, you get a very realistic explosion that wraps itself around the ships.

"We took the miniature 'boxes' out into the deepest, darkest night when it was bitterly cold," Gajdecki remembers, "suspended them about 150 feet up from a construction crane, then detonated the charges. Two cameras — one 120 fps and another 500 fps [frames per second] were shooting upwards from the safety of crash boxes underneath the explosions. By filming from directly below, you get a zero gravity look, where the fire and debris careers out evenly in all directions. In space, of course, there is no gravity, so we didn't want the blast material to fall straight down. We also blew up some models on the ground, to be used for the close-ups of the ships colliding." As spectacular as the final shots were when they appeared on screen months later, the immediate effect in the night skies above Toronto at the time was pretty crowd-pleasing too. "Oliver Stone was shooting a film a couple of fields along from us that night," Gajdecki grins, "and

all his crew stopped to come and watch what we were doing. I thought that was pretty cool."

Above: Kaboom! Hours of preparation pay off.

Spaceships of another kind kept James Tichenor and his team fully occupied for days during the 'Thor's Chariot' episode. "The major sequence with the ship coming out of the sky was *so* hard to do," he says. "This was only my third show as full supervisor without any help or guidance from my mentor Gajdecki, and it was a pretty radical amount of work for me to tackle at the time. A lot of the ship emerging from the clouds was something that, in a big budget movie, would have been done using models, but on a TV budget we didn't have that luxury. So we did it all CG. The artists at GVFX in Toronto spent almost a full week working twenty to twenty-two hours a day to get this sequence, and there are only four or five shots in it! The scene with the clouds unwrapping is all hand animated, carefully manipulated to make it look as real as possible. We even had some of the clouds running backwards to increase the turbulence effect. Another tricky thing for them was to get the sense of scale right. We had the ship, which is supposed to be about a mile long, next to some pyramids sitting on a hill, and we added tiny little people all around, so trying to scale it and

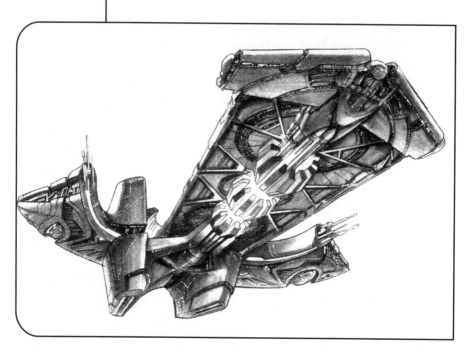

Above: A production drawing of Thor's ship, as seen in 'Thor's Chariot'.

Opposite page: The intricate Death Glider models have a two foot wingspan, and are shot against a greenscreen using a motion control camera.

make everything look really big was extremely difficult. Whilst the sequence is astounding, Tichenor still feels there is much he would change if he had the opportunity to recreate the effect. "The concept of the pyramids being sucked away by the beams from Thor's ship is just so big! I wanted to see them breaking apart, with pieces flying off and disintegrating before disappearing, but you can only do so much in so little time. When Jon Glassner first told us about it, I thought 'Holy Smoke! Is this a feature film we're talking about or an episode for television?' To give them credit, the producers really pushed for it, and were confident we were going to be able to achieve it."

Of all the incredible effects created for seasons one and two, the episode dearest to Tichenor's heart is 'Serpent's Song', not just because the effects were so good, but "because I got to meet and work with [director] Peter DeLuise. He is truly a great guy and an inspiration." Visual effects-wise, Tichenor suggests, "In a way it was kind of recreating what we did in 'In the Line of Duty', where we had the Death Gliders scraping the beach and blowing things up. This time we went to a desert location and, though there were very few explosions, it contains one of my all time favourite shots. There is one scene where O'Neill stops and looks, and then we cut to the Glider turning and settling into place ready to shoot him, and he

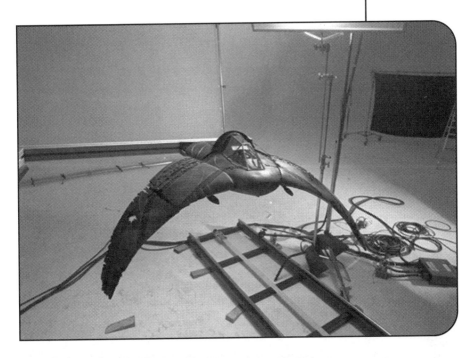

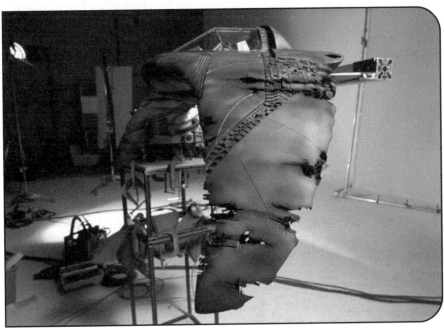

Above: Preparing one of the bugs from 'Show and Tell'.

manages to back into the Gate just as it fires. We do this one continuous shot where the camera pulls back through the Stargate then travels backwards along the wormhole and comes out on the other side with O'Neill. He gets up and the iris closes. I *love* that shot, because it has so many different angles. It had the Glider turning, the Glider shooting, all the Stargate effects as you pass through it, and then the iris closing. It was a great shot to do and I never tire of watching it!"

Whilst most of us look forward to a good night's sleep, the people who create the special visual effects for *Stargate SG-1* are more likely to be sneaking around alleyways blowing up bags of dog food. Certainly, John Gajdecki is, and he isn't the least bit embarrassed to admit it. Using the fact that he greatly admires Peter DeLuise as an excuse, he shrugs, "We wanted to create some extra special explosions for another one of Peter DeLuise's episodes. In 'Show and Tell' there are several scenes where invisible aliens are trying to kill the guys in Stargate Command, and the SG guys shoot and destroy them. After lots of trials and consultations we came up with the idea of using dog food mixed with some other goop [serious technical term] to represent these giant bugs' innards." Gajdecki explains

that it took more than twelve hours in the dark, in an alley outside the workshops to film the explosions that would be added to CG effects to show the bugs exploding. "We had to create 3D bugs that were invisible most of the time but which could be illuminated by a special weapon donated by the Tok'ra, and when we can see these things we can kill them. When they're shot they explode, and to achieve the VFX, we built physical models of the bugs and filled them with our magic mixture and some small explosives. We then hung the models, marionette style, in the correct orientation and let 'em blow!"

Speaking on behalf of all the talented artists that create the special visual effects for the series, Tichenor concludes, "This is a very exciting show to work on and be part of. We have really solid producers who keep the momentum going, and we work with some great people. Every week, we are trying to make the audience feel that they are going to new places, or experiencing what it's like to go through the Stargate. We're always trying to figure out ways of making the impact more subjective for the audience, to make it more emotional." With a shelf-full of awards to their credit, the VFX wizards of *Stargate SG-1* have been more than successful. ⋏

Above: The bugs were suspended marionette style and filled with dog food, before being blown up!

Make-up

Jonathan Glassner

"Without a doubt, we have some of the best make-up artists in North America on our team."

Jan Newman initially took on the role of make-up supervisor on *Stargate SG-1* with some reluctance. "I had been working on features mostly and didn't want to do episodic work for a while. However, when it transpired that Richard Dean Anderson and Michael Greenburg [who she had got to know on *MacGyver*] had specifically asked for me, I couldn't turn it down. I would crawl over broken glass for them." First, she rented a copy of the movie because "I wanted to create a look specially for *Stargate SG-1*, but needed to get a 'feel' of what had been done previously." But there was still a surprise to come for Newman and her team. "When we signed on we thought it was all going to be pretty straightforward, but when we

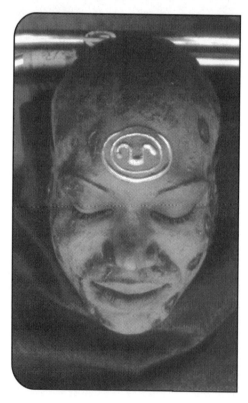

turned up for the pilot... There was a multitude of extra cast members and they were far from ordinary. We had aliens in the most fabulous costumes, so we designed special eye make-up to enhance the effect."

For Newman, the collaboration between the art directors, costume and special prosthetic make-up artists to create the helmet structure for Apophis and his Jaffa was particularly pleasing. "Moulds were taken of the actors' heads so that the capped helmets would fit snugly. Then they were made to resemble impenetrable armour and given this wonderful sheen. It was all a major pain in the backside to recreate that for each individual at the time, but to see them all marching along together was truly amazing."

Newman's crew's initial solution for creating the distinctive forehead mark of Apophis's serpent guard was a rubber stamp, "but it didn't work because everyone's forehead is different. So then we tried to stencil it on by cutting out the design and adding tattoo colour." Thankfully, technological advancements soon made the process far easier and quicker. "The art department creates the design on computer and produces a peel-off vinyl transfer which we stick on and then cover with silicone based paint. Now the tattoo stays on all day even with the vagaries of our Vancouver weather."

Stargate SG-1's normally patient make-up supremo does admit to one particularly challenging aspect of her job, but it also makes her laugh every day. "Christopher Judge!" she grins. "He has such a rambunctious nature that it's a challenge keeping his make-up in place. If he jumps into a vehicle or ducks into a trailer on set; to simply brush his head on the doorframe means we have to re-create his look. He's very high maintenance, but utterly charming with it." Still, Newman is grateful that Teal'c's make-up isn't more complex. "Originally, Teal'c was supposed to look more like the stylised version of an Egyptian. He started out with long, droopy, prosthetic ears and had a long, braided beard like the depictions of the Pharaohs. He would have looked spectacular and it was a wonderful concept, but when I saw it I just groaned, because I thought about how difficult it would be to keep that look on a day-to-day, minute-to-minute basis." Newman says Wright's and Glassner's decision to go with the present look was "one of the best they made."

If Teal'c is high maintenance, Jack O'Neill is high speed. "The biggest thing with Richard Dean Anderson is getting him to sit still long enough for us to get him ready for camera!" Newman laughs. "He has a very short attention span, and all he wants to do is come in, get it done and move on to the rest of his day."

When pushed for particular make-up favourites, Jan says that for her and her assistants Margaret and Christopher, "Richard's Neanderthal look in 'The Broca Divide' and old-age make-up from 'Brief Candle' are the ones we talk about most."

Opposite page: Teal'c's boils and blisters in 'Bane'. Above: An aged O'Neill in 'Brief Candle'.

Costume Design

Christina McQuarrie

"Most of the people we clothe are misplaced humans from ancient cultures, which have evolved in a slightly different way. That's where we come in. We find the tricks to make them recognisable and give a flavour of that culture."

"I can't explain how I fell into becoming senior designer for *Stargate SG-1*," laughs a modest Christine McQuarrie, "but I am very glad I did." Anyone who has ever marvelled at the variety, intricacy and sheer volume of the designs created by the lady would be more than happy to explain the reason for her appointment. From Egyptian goddesses to medieval villagers, McQuarrie and her team have consistently produced a breathtaking array of garments that put *Stargate SG-1* in a league of its own. Coming from a theatrical background, McQuarrie had been tempted into the costume departments of various high flying series, practising her art on numerous science fiction shows before being invited to work her magic on *Stargate SG-1*.

"I came on board pleading for them not to make me do aliens," she smiles, "not because I don't like aliens, but because my first love is period costume. I enjoy making and building things from scratch, and didn't feel I knew that much about the dress habits of weirder beings from other planets!" However, during the first two years, McQuarrie and her team wholeheartedly threw themselves into the learning process and came to love the idea of creating outfits for 'out of towners'. "It's not as stressful as I thought and can actually be a lot of fun," she points out. "Sometimes the aliens get created by our special effects department, but a lot of the time we just come up with an idea, and more often than not the writers will tell us to go ahead."

McQuarrie's first foray into the *Stargate* universe could have been terrifying for a lesser mortal, but her experience in manufacturing classic garments helped tremendously when it came to designing the original pieces for the show. The première episode, 'Children

of the Gods', required around 200 costumes from different historical eras. "I used the *Stargate* film as a starting point, and then was inspired solely by visual interest," she explains. "By mixing modern fabrics with classic designs from Egypt, Rome, Assyria and the like, I was able to create costumes that gave a feeling of a particular society or time period without taking too many historical liberties. We didn't want the clothes to be too closely identified with any actual Earth culture, because they were meant to have been developed on different planets at different times. It wouldn't have worked had they been exactly like the clothes worn by our ancient Egyptians for example, but I did want to suggest the right kind of ambience."

The process starts for the costume design crew very early on. "We get the script, read it and try to envisage what the writers would like. I'm not that great at drawing," insists McQuarrie, who claims she has to spend hours labouring over her own drawings whilst the wonders in the production design art department sail through theirs. Her inspiration comes from all quarters: "I use reference books, paintings, sculpture, even the markings on a piece of driftwood can set me thinking!" Λ

Opposite page:
Costume sketch for a
Dignitary.
Above (left): *A*
Tollan Guard.
Above: *The original*
design sketch for
Bra'tac's costume.

Stargate and the Fans

Don S. Davis

"The fans took the seed of an idea, planted it, and out of that grew Gatecon."

It used to be that fans, especially fans of science fiction shows, were given a seriously bad deal. Classed as 'geeks' and 'anoraks', no self-respecting studio or network executive would have been seen sharing so much as a glass of sparkling water with them. However, about a month before *Stargate SG-1* was first screened, the US cable channel Showtime and MGM Worldwide Television launched an interactive companion to the series on the World Wide Web. It allowed visitors to view the site through a 3-D image of the Stargate, and get a head start on the characters and the content of the show. At the time, Jeff Morris, Showtime's vice president of New Media Technology and Development, announced, "The site has been designed to encourage active viewer participation, which will add a new dimension of excitement to what we expect to be a breakthrough television series."

Initially, all of the content for the website was produced by Showtime's New Media division, in conjunction with MGM Worldwide Television's boffins, and the site at *stargatesg-1.com* is still one of the most comprehensive and challenging on the Internet. Such was the enthusiasm for the new show that hundreds of fan-run websites sprung up within weeks, and soon the *Stargate SG-1* webring was offering a comprehensive list of every sort of site, encompassing technology-based information and shrines honouring individual members of the cast and crew. Some were pretty dire, others fairly spectacular, offering better design concepts and more diverse information than the 'official' webmasters had ever dreamed possible. And the 'official' webmasters were taking notes. Jonathan Glassner, a sneaky regular to

some of the sites, thought "some of the unofficial sites were awesome." Sean Fitzgibbons, a seventeen year-old computer whiz, was convinced he'd trodden on a few well-shod toes when MGM contacted him to discuss his site. "I thought for sure they were going to shut me down," he recalls. "I certainly didn't expect them to ask me to run a site for them!" Inspired by Sean's expertise with *SG1.Net* — a site he put together in collaboration with many other *SG-1* webmasters — MGM made him a consultant. The action served to convey just how important fan activity was to the management's overall assessment of the show.

As well as affording the opportunity for marketing *SG-1* goods (some of the best merchandise is available only at MGM's site: *Stargate-SG1.com*), the internet gave the programme-makers a chance to gauge fan reactions. As Brad Wright explains, "I'm often asked if various things in the show have been written in response to fans' ideas or preferences. Actually what happens is, because we're working so far ahead and have finished an episode ten or twelve weeks before the fans see it, their comments are a great indication of whether or not we're getting it right. Often we'll see a post from someone saying

Opposite page: The show has enjoyed a hugely successful video and DVD release.

Above: Left to right: Kim Cowan, Thomasina Gibson, Julie Connolly and Richard Dean Anderson, all working hard on location for 'Dead Man's Switch'.

'wouldn't it be great if…' and we have a little smile to ourselves knowing that it's exactly what *is* going to happen several episodes down the line." Sometimes things don't go down so well, and the programme-makers can see that too. Some fans can get a trifle carried away with their enthusiasm for various characters, and Wright had to step in on one occasion to allay fears that a new female character on the show was going to run off with Jack O'Neill!

Television and the media are careful fan watchers. SKY One, the first network to air *Stargate SG-1* in the UK, actively encourage fans to have their say and have invited viewers to comment on the show via their interactive web-site and by phone. A recent clash-of-the-titans type poll received hundreds of thousands of votes and placed *Stargate SG-1* and *Star Trek* neck and neck for the top spot for several weeks.

'Gatewatchers' don't just sit in front of their screens all day and night. Thousands of them actually meet to talk about the show face to face. The smallest gatherings are called 'mini-cons', where a few people get together to watch some episodes and either drool or nit-pick, depending on how many chocolate milkshakes have been consumed. Much larger are the specialist conventions where hundreds converge to meet stars from the show, learn more about the production process first hand, team up with other like-minded souls and, most importantly, raise money for charitable causes. Conventions like SG-2 in London and the innovative *Gatecon* in Vancouver have raised tens of thousands of pounds for worthy causes internationally. Actor Christopher Judge was particularly touched when a recipient from the *Make a Wish Foundation* (an organisation created to bring special times to seriously ill children and their families) got up to talk about her experience with *SG-1*. Her dearest wish had been to see her dog in an episode of her favourite show, a wish the programme-makers were happy to grant. Look out for him in 'Singularity'.

"I was astounded at the knowledge, expertise, professionalism and sheer enthusiasm of the people who put our Vancouver convention together," producer John Smith concludes. "It makes you realise how much people appreciate what we're doing with this show." **Λ**

Opposite page: Gatecon 2000: Don S. Davis entertains the fans (top), and Teryl Rothery's photo of a very happy audience (bottom). Above: A fan's dearest wish fulfilled. O'Neill, Cassie and furry friend in 'Singularity'.

Afterword

would love to say that *Stargate SG-1*'s success is due to our skills as producers. But the truth is, our biggest skill was picking an amazingly talented cast and crew and convincing them to come play with us. Sure, we dreamed up some pretty fantastic stuff on paper, but people like production designer Richard Hudolin, who was the first person we begged to come on board, realised them. Richard and his team are responsible for the rich, magical look of the show — the sets, the costumes and the props all came from the fertile imaginations of Richard and his staff. And we were blessed to have been working with a man named John Gajdecki, visual effects maven, on *The Outer Limits*. He and James Tichenor stepped onto *Stargate* for the pilot and the first season (James stayed on after that) and set the tone for a show that I believe has been setting the standards for visual effects on television ever since. All of these people, with their "can do" attitudes, freed me, Brad and all our writers to imagine anything and put it on paper.

And we were lucky... boy were we lucky. We not only had amazing people working for us, but we worked for amazing people. John

Symes made perhaps the biggest contribution with one phone call to Brad and me. John's opening sentence went like this: "Hey guys, what would you think of Jack O'Neill being played by Richard Dean Anderson?"

Richard Dean Anderson *is* Jack O'Neill; Jack O'Neill *is* Richard Dean Anderson. As Brad and I conceived him, he was different from the Jack O'Neill of the movie — he was more alive, a lot less spit and polish military, and he had a sense of humour. That sense of humour is as much Rick as it is the writers. He's funny. He's also a pleasure to work with. He imbues the set with one of his mottoes — 'Life's too short'. So the mood on the set, even in the most stressful situations (like in a frozen ice cave or a massive storm), was always one of fun.

Opposite page: SG-1 *on the lookout for trouble in* 'Cold Lazarus'. *Above:* Jonathan Glassner.

And of course the rest of the cast — Michael Shanks, Amanda Tapping, Christopher Judge, Don Davis and Teryl Rothery — well what can I say? These are people you want to invite into your living room for an hour every week. They are the heart and soul of *Stargate SG-1* and, I believe, the main reason millions of people tune in around the world to see the show.

I could go on listing the many people responsible for this show (like John Smith, the best line producer I know; or Robert Cooper, the writer/producer who saved us many times) but this Afterword would start to sound like an awards show speech. Suffice it to say that none of us did it alone.

As you've read this book, I'm sure that it has come across that those of us who worked on *Stargate SG-1* were very fortunate people, indeed. After all — we got to play in the greatest sandbox of our lives.

Jonathan Glassner
Executive Producer/Co-creator *Stargate SG-1*
May 2001

Above: Two Ts having a titter on location during the filming of 'Dead Man's Switch'.

Thomasina Gibson trained as a primary school teacher, but decided to follow her first love of theatre by moving to Stratford Upon Avon and working at the Royal Shakespeare Theatre. She then assuaged her wanderlust by travelling the world as a cabin crew member for British Airways. Joining the BBC, she worked in radio and television for several years before becoming a full time mum. She returned to writing five years ago, deciding to specialise in a major passion, cult television and films. She now writes for the majority of UK film and television magazines, plus several printed and on-line publications in the US and Canada, and has contributed to mainstream newspapers including the *Daily Telegraph* and London *Evening Standard*. She has worked as a consultant on several sci-fi/cult related television shows, including the BBC's *Lost in Space* series and Channel 4's factual documentary *Riddle of the Skies*. She recently worked as director/associate producer for MGM on added value contributions for the *Stargate SG-1* DVDs. Gibson is currently working with Terry James (*Tess of the D'Urbevilles*, *Children of the New Forest*) on a young persons' sci-fi adventure television series. Å